Mortal E

Mortal Beings

Carl Lombard

FOURTH ESTATE · *London*

First published in Great Britain in 1993 by
Fourth Estate Limited
289 Westbourne Grove
London W11 2QA

A catalogue record for this book is available from the British
Library.

ISBN 1–85702–103–7

Typeset by York House Typographic Ltd, London
Printed in Great Britain by Biddles Ltd, Guildford

For
Joan and David Lombard
and
Yvonne

Chapter One

No one could say when it had begun. Even the old women who had long ago buried their husbands could only testify that ever since they were young themselves the family had always included a plethora of aged aunts who had outlived their menfolk by twenty or thirty years. The regular intake of new blood through marriage had made no difference: and it was spoken of as tradition rather than science, a duty which befell the men once they had spawned a clutch of children and reached the age of menopause, to simply die and leave the women to fend for themselves.

Sinead Bean Uí Carthaigh was standing in the scullery of her house washing out the demijohns in which she had made apple wine the previous autumn. Since then there had been several large gatherings, some occasioned by the usual depletion amongst the men. Another two of them had died and three infants had been christened in the same year, all of which had taken their toll on the brew she had set aside in the hope that it would last a number of years. Nothing about her day so far had been unusual. She rose at half past six and made potato cakes and oatmeal to feed herself and the only son still living with her. At eight o'clock her daughter Bridget came down, full of joy and

1

singing to herself, and washed her face in the copper handbasin. In answer to her mother's questions about the reason for her excessive good humour, Bridget insisted that it was nothing more than a natural reaction to the warmth of the morning and the prospect that the good weather would continue until the weekend, meaning she could picnic for two days with Darius on the mountain. Before she left her mother, the girl put her arms around the ageing woman and assured her, as she had done on several occasions during the previous few days, that she loved her intensely. With that she went out the door and was singing again by the time she reached the gate.

There was no question but that Sinead Bean Uí Carthaigh was impressed by her daughter's display of affection. It was very much in the nature of the girl to begin each day with a burst of enthusiasm, but her behaviour that morning had been enlightened beyond what was normal and this was why her mother, as she stood washing the demijohns in her scullery, brimmed with the expectation that Bridget would soon return with Darius and inform her that she wished to marry the young bookkeeper. Sinead Bean Uí Carthaigh's particular frame of mind was such that she felt more and more certain as the day progressed that she was right in this forecast.

The ageing woman had not yet finished cleaning the demijohns when her daughter turned the door-handle and entered the kitchen with Darius. Then Bridget entered the scullery and asked her mother to join them in the larger room. When she did so, the young couple informed her that they wished to be married and asked if she knew of any reason why they should not be. This was not a new situation for Sinead Bean Uí Carthaigh. She had faced it three times before, as one by one her children left her. This may explain the intuition which had possessed her all of that day . . . but that is of no real importance. Before she was willing to give her consent she asked to be left alone with the bookkeeper for a short time, so Bridget left the room, her happy mood somewhat tempered by apprehension.

What Sinead Bean Uí Carthaigh had to say to Darius was not to be taken lightly. It would be no exaggeration to say that it was a lecture about life and death itself. She asked the young man if he had noticed that there was a dearth of elderly men in the family. He replied that he had, but that this was of no concern to him as he was of different blood. At this he was cut short by Sinead Bean Uí Carthaigh, who placed her hand over his mouth to stop it speaking in such a way. 'That's of no consequence,' she said to him. 'Don't even think in such a way again. There have, if truth be known, always been more females than males born into this family. As each of them has married, new blood has been introduced. But you were at the christening of Bernadette Olive Bridget in February and again at the christening of Patricia Niamh Deirdre Bridget in April, and between those two events two more men died. Neither of them was of our blood, so don't ever believe, Darius, that your own blood is a protection. It is not. You may have my daughter's hand in marriage but I have said what it is my duty to say. It is for you to decide now.'

It was to be another year before Bridget and Darius married. By the time they did, there had been two more christenings, both of baby girls, and another death. This time it was Maol Mhuile Nocton, who had fallen from a ladder while cleaning the eaves of his terracotta whiskey shed. The doctors said that his demise was due to a fractured skull, but his wife was supported by

3

the other women in the private assertion that Maol Mhuile Nocton was dead by the time his head hit the gravel. Everything about his life had suggested he was ready for such a departure. He had reared six children. He had reached the limits of his potential as a violinist with the city orchestra. And he was at the right age for the menopause. In short, it was time for him to go. His wife had no doubts that the diagnosis offered by the doctors was nothing but a ploy to divert attention from the fact that they could not explain this chronic phenomenon. But this was no cause for complaint from the family, none of whom had expected Maol Mhuile Nocton to do any different at his age.

Ten months after their wedding day, Bridget and Darius Gaynor had their first child. In the months preceding the child's birth, Bridget Gaynor had engaged in a process of quiet attrition aimed at persuading her husband that, should the child be a boy, he should be named after the first Pope. During the pregnancy the couple were noted for public displays of certainty that the child would be male; however, this bravado concealed a private fear that it would not. They resorted to clandestine visits to druids in the hope that from their array of archaic techniques of foresight, including those of a blind Carpathian who based her prognosis on the farts of the mother, there would emerge a consensus of prediction. But there was no consensus among the soothsayers and so the couple had no option but to wait and let nature take its course, which it did on 15 August, when Bridget Gaynor gave birth to a boy who was hastily christened Peadar.

Only five months after the birth of Peadar the couple found they were expecting a second child. Without telling her husband, Bridget Gaynor slipped from their house one evening and went to see Father Adrian

McManus, who was quietly enjoying a glass of whiskey when he was disturbed by a knock on the presbytery door. There stood Bridget Gaynor, who informed him that she had come in search of an historical fact which she was sure he would be happy to provide. She was shown into what the priest described as his study, which was nothing more than the room where he ate his bacon sandwiches in the mornings, drank his whiskey in the evenings and composed his monotonous sermons on Saturday afternoons. In addition, the room housed a library consisting of eighteen latin manuscripts, few of which Father Adrian McManus could remember reading. 'What is it I can do for you?' he said to the woman, ushering her to the dusty armchair by the window.

Bridget Gaynor began by saying that she had come on her own behalf and that her husband knew nothing of the visit, and that she would appreciate it if things remained that way. The priest agreed and asked again the reason for her presence, so she continued. What Bridget Gaynor had come to discuss with the priest was her growing desire to continue to name her sons after the succession of Popes. She had not yet said a word of this to her husband, but she felt that such a gesture would be some requital for the good fortune she had enjoyed for most of her life. Although she did not know the gender of her second child (no further visits had been made to clairvoyants) her intention was to prepare herself in the event that it would be another boy. 'You see, Father,' she said to him, 'I have no idea who succeeded Peadar as Pope, and I would be most grateful if you could tell me.'

It was an embarrassing ordeal for the priest, for he had no idea of the answer. In his haste to disguise the fact by jumping from his chair as if remembering a

5

pressing engagement, he spilt the remainder of his whiskey over his cassock. 'My good woman,' he said, 'this is all very worthy of you and I would be happy to answer your question when you have considered the matter further and, I think, perhaps in conjunction with your husband. When you have both thought it over and are agreed that this is your wish, then return to me and I will tell you what you want to know. Now you must excuse me, but I have a sermon to compose.'

The evening that Bridget Gaynor went to have her hair permed, the rain came down with such intensity that it bent the gutters which Darius Gaynor had installed a week before. Such rain was a terrible sight from the inside of Monica Fitzgibbons's kitchen, where the women went to have their hair done. From there it was a five-minute walk to the house of Darius and Bridget Gaynor, plenty of time for Monica Fitzgibbons's handywork to be destroyed by the downpour. Bridget Gaynor squinted out the window up at the sky, but there were no impending breaks in the cloud which might give her a chance to get home dry, so she tightened the scarf about her head to a tension she thought would leave the creation intact, pulled the door open and raced across the street towards the butcher's canopy opposite. From there she ran between the porches and the awnings like a cat burglar, all the time getting closer to her house. When she arrived she stood nervously in front of the mirror set into the coatstand and removed the covering from her head, revealing the new exhibit to be in perfect condition.

As she lay in bed that night, with several towels rolled up and wedged behind her neck to keep her head off the pillow, Darius lay beside her staring at the ceiling. Despite his wife's state of early pregnancy, he decided that it might be permissible to run his hands over her body and grope at this and that. He moved his right hand across the sheet, but as soon as she was aware of its progress she dismissed it immediately with a 'Phsssssst!' sound blown from the side of her mouth. It was no more than Darius had expected. Bridget Gaynor was always like this after a visit to see Monica Fitzgibbons, a woman who was credited with the invention of a unique kind of birth control, as sex was never permitted on the night of a new hairdo. As they lay in their glamour-imposed chastity, Bridget Gaynor told her husband of her desire to name the new child after the second Pope, should it be a boy. She told him that she had been to see Father Adrian McManus, and asked her husband if he would accompany her when she went back to the priest for the name of the man in question.

Seven weeks after Bridget Gaynor had gone to the presbytery, Father Adrian McManus had managed to have his cassock cleaned, and had received a reply to a letter sent to Father Richard T. O'Sullivan who had been a contemporary of his at the national seminary and whose interest in religious history was second only to his love of Graeco-Roman wrestling. However, it would be no exaggeration to say that Father Adrian McManus was surprised to open his front door and find Darius and Bridget Gaynor standing in the fog. Seven weeks was a long time in the life of this priest, and he had presumed a month before that the woman who had come to him on such an unusual quest had either grown cold to the idea or been refused permission to pursue it by her husband when she broached the subject with him. But there they stood, all smiling and nervous. The priest showed them into his study, where Bridget Gaynor wasted no time in seating herself again in the dusty armchair.

Father Adrian McManus went to the shelf which contained six of his books (he spread them around to make it appear that he had more than was the case) and from one of them he pulled a piece of paper which had been inserted like a bookmark. 'Now,' he said to them, 'I have some good news for you, but I'm afraid that I also have some bad news for you. First the good. I have been able to find the information you requested. The bad news is that I am not sure if this is a good idea, especially if you decide to continue beyond the second son.' The priest went on to inform them that the name of the second Pope was Linus, who had in AD 67 succeeded Peter to the office which would in time bestow on his successors such a splendid line of titles: Bishop of Rome, Vicar of Christ, Successor of the Apostles, Pontifex Maximus of the Universal Church, Patriarch of the West, Primate of Italy, Archbishop and Metropolitan of the Province of Rome, State Sovereign of the Vatican City and Servant of the Servants of God. He suggested that, while a name like Linus was not too much of a burden and did lend itself to nicknames such as Lino or Linny, if they were to continue to follow a nomenclature based on a line of ancient fishermen then they could make life a trial for their future sons. For the third Pope was called Anacletus, and his successors corresponding to what Father Adrian McManus considered to be within the fertility potential of a Catholic womb included Evaristus (fifth), Hyginus (ninth), Eleutherius (thirteenth) and Zephyrinus (fifteenth). But Bridget Gaynor had heard all she wanted to know and was in no doubt that Linus would indeed be a good name. In the months which followed, she took to pacing up and down in front of her hearth when she was alone, with her hands resting on her stomach, repeating the words 'Be a boy, be a boy,' and on an autumn night somewhere between a quarter to eight and a quarter past, Linus Gaynor was born.

For thirteen more years, Darius and Bridget Gaynor continued to have children with expected regularity. In all there were another six – two boys and four girls. But the practice of naming the boys after the papal succession was relaxed to the extent that the others were called Pius and John. The family lived comfortably, due in large part to the excellent financial skills of Darius Gaynor, who practised the thrift that he preached. They ate well and were unafflicted by ill-health – until the day that Walter Love rapped on her door and told Bridget Gaynor that she must come quickly. They drove to a creamery a mile away, where he led her to an ugly hut at the back of the yard. Inside she found a number of people gathered around a desk. None of them was doing anything; they all just stood looking down at the back of the head of Darius Gaynor, who lay slumped across an ominous balance sheet with his pen still in his hand. He had been forty-nine, and Bridget Gaynor sent out word that the old women again had reason to gather.

No one had ever considered it at all important for any of the young men of the family to go to university. The idea of them spending years in deep study (for that was their picture of student life) seemed cruel, given the limited period of time they would have in which to enjoy the fruits of such exertion. It was not that anyone had anything against universities, but no pressure was ever brought to bear on anyone to embark on academic study. So it was with Linus Gaynor. His youth was spent playing one sport after another – he excelled in particular at goalkeeping, and played for several soccer teams. Soaring into the air above his fellow players made him happy, and he had a way, it seemed, of defying gravity and staying airborne for long periods of time. Speaking of him later, one of his team-mates remarked that he did not so much jump as levitate, taking in the view as he did so before returning to earth. This ability placed him in great demand, for a goalkeeper was always hard to find, let alone a good one.

It was while keeping goal that Linus Gaynor became such a jester. Around his posts small groups of people would gather to talk to him. There he would regale them with jokes and sometimes songs, interrupting himself occasionally to leap into the air and catch the ball. When he came down he would ask to be reminded of where he had got to in his story, then continue. If he was not soaring about or talking to people at his goal-posts, he might be playing poker. Gambling for money in a public house was illegal, as was the presence of anyone under sixteen, but no one paid any heed. In the summer they would even take the tables out into the street to play, in full view of the local police station.

None of this was any kind of preparation for an academic life. His mother never made an issue of it – she was concerned only that he should learn to read and write with some degree of competence, and beyond that she did not much mind. Linus Gaynor did learn to read and write, and he also remained in school until he was seventeen. This was not because he had any ambition to go to university: it was simply the easiest thing for him to do. Since he was fourteen he had always shunned any decision about his future life, and staying in school was a good way of continuing this. When he had no alternative but to leave, he did so with heavy heart, prolonging the exercise by going to the beautiful City University to sit its entrance examination.

It was one hour into his first examination, on chemistry, that the invigilator rang the bell which meant that those who wished to leave could do so. Though most of the questions were completely incomprehensible to him, Linus Gaynor continued to sit for some time after the bell to enjoy observing those for whom the whole exercise was a matter of immense importance. From time to time he would catch the official's eye, wink at him and raise his eyebrows as if in consternation at the questions he was being asked to answer. He had sat like this for twenty minutes or so, when his attention was taken by a young woman with short black hair and sallow skin who sat across from him and ten seats in front. She made a small fuss as she gathered her belongings together and walked to the desk where she handed her paper to the invigilator without even looking at him. She then went to the door and closed it quietly behind her. A minute later Linus Gaynor did likewise.

The following day he returned to sit a second examination. This time it was on accountancy, about which he knew even less than chemistry, his father having failed to inculcate in his second son his own fascination at the redoubtable honesty of mathematics. 'A number is the most loyal friend you will ever have,' he would say to his children as he corrected their homework. 'A number will never tell you a lie.'

During the first compulsory hour Linus Gaynor did not even bother to read the questions, for he knew that to do so would be a waste of time. Instead he simply stared across at the young woman who had left before him the previous day and of whom he now had a clear view when everyone else had their heads down writing. His position was ideal, because he could look at her constantly without her noticing, and he gazed at her for an hour. Not since he had seen Nelson Nelson, his goalkeeping hero, when Darius Gaynor had taken him to his first international soccer match had Linus Gaynor been so mesmerised by another human being.

The sequence of the previous day repeated itself. After an hour the invigilator rang his little bell, and some twenty minutes later there was a small fuss as the female student gathered her things and left the hall. This time Linus Gaynor followed her more closely. He made no attempt to speak to her but simply trailed her for a time, as this was the first chance he had to see her in any setting but the examination hall. She was shorter than he, and his eyes were drawn to her bottom, which was slightly large but certainly attractively so. She walked down the main boulevard of the campus, past the red-hot pokers, the flowering onions and the bleeding hearts, and then cut across the grass to shorten the journey to the gate, walking beneath the sweet chestnuts and the Japanese larches. When she arrived at the footpath outside, she crossed the road and waited for a bus. From where he lay on the burnt lawn, Linus Gaynor watched her mount a bus and disappear into a group of passengers. Then he went home himself, thinking that this examination business was a pretty entertaining thing to do.

Throughout the week things did not change at all. Her timing was precise, leaving twenty minutes after the little bell. Linus Gaynor sat through mathematical formulas, geological faults and French verbs without noticing any of them. At one stage the invigilator caught him by surprise and asked him if he did not think he was wasting his time turning up. 'Nonsense,' replied Linus Gaynor. 'I'm merely waiting for the religion examination. Then you'll see me write until the very end as if my hand was guided by John the Evangelist.' There was, of course, no such thing as a religion exam – at least not at that level – but that was of no matter except to confirm to the invigilator that the student who had barely written his name all week was nothing but a dunderhead.

The day which was to prove significant for Linus Gaynor was that on which the students' knowledge of Latin was tested. Not that he had much to test, but he did possess a thorough memory of an English translation of *De Bello Gallico* and so he surprised the examining official by writing intently for half an hour as he quickly, and completely accurately, translated a section of Caesar's book. But this was not why the day was to be significant, although his academic efforts exceeded those in the rest of his week combined. The significance of the day was caused by the events which took place at one of the Japanese larches when he finally caught up with the girl with the slightly large bottom and told her that he had once heard an American tourist tell her companions as they passed the university gardens that what they were looking at was the botanical gardens. The girl showed no interest in this piece of information and continued to walk to the gate. Nor was she impressed by Linus Gaynor's tales of goalkeeping heroism, even ignoring his long leap into the air to demonstrate his technique. Nothing made her stop walking until he told her that he was likely to die when he was no more than fifty. 'What makes you say such a thing,' she said to him.

'How do you know the moon will rise tonight?' he answered – 'Because it's nature. And nature is the most

13

loyal friend you will ever have, because it will never tell you a lie.'

This was not the first time that Linus Gaynor had used the promise of his early demise to attract the attention of a woman. He had discovered during the previous two years that the desire to give comfort was a primary one in a woman, and the story he had to tell was one which elicited such actions without fail. At least that had been the case with the eight previous young women he had tried it on, and so he regarded his inheritance as a thick silver lining with a minute black cloud at the centre. Not for him the hours of mawkish foreboding which had turned his elder brother into a boorish man: for Linus Gaynor, fate was a reel with which to drag people towards him – not in a sinister way, but just to make them pay attention to him when he spoke. He had often used the line, 'I'm going to die when I'm fifty, so be quiet and listen to me.' The moral authority which this gave him was irresistible, and standing beneath the Japanese larches he called on it again to make the girl with the slightly large bottom stop and talk to him.

During the following months Linus Gaynor and Gretchen Murray paid many visits to the mountain where his family's lovers had gone for generations. It was there that they grew to love each other, gradually increasing their familiarity with each other's body. The excitement of this time was in no way disturbed by the arrival of the examination results. Gretchen Murray had failed to pass anything. Linus Gaynor fared even worse, his results being annotated with an enquiry as to why he should want to waste the authorities' time. The extent of his growing feeling for the young woman was most evident in the way it affected his concentration at those pastimes which had previously been so effortless for him. Now when he soared between the goalposts he regularly found that his timing was incorrect, sometimes landing again before the ball flew over his head, sometimes rising too late to make his rendezvous. His team-mates began to grow impatient with him as their league position deteriorated and they made early exits from competitions. Even at poker he began to take heavy losses, gambling money on paltry hands and running into debt. But none of this mattered to him as he grew to realise he had so much with which to replace it.

As so many of his ancestors had had to do – at least those with any conscience – Linus Gaynor gradually brought home to Gretchen Murray the reality of what he had first told her beneath the Japanese larches. She confessed that at first she thought he was not serious and had only stopped because she was impressed by such a bold introduction. But as the weeks passed, and in small episodes of earnestness, he began to acquaint her fully with the danger which lurked inside him. That he believed he had still another thirty years or so was certainly a comfort, but that was but a minor consideration in their ever closer friendship and then love. The true reason why they continued to grow in love with each other was the ancient adage about living like a lion for a day, and they felt that though their time together would be limited, it would indeed be far better than a considered retreat based on what was going to happen in three decades' time.

The orchard at the edge of the town which had for so long supplied the ingredients for the family's wine was razed the year before. The trees had been plagued by apple canker and no amount of pesticides or witchcraft had been able to cure them, so Bridget Gaynor had reluctantly ordered them cut down and burnt lest the disease spread. The field was now abandoned and the grass had grown long around the low stumps where once there had been such a clatter of laughing and singing in the autumn harvest. Bridget Gaynor now turned her attention to elderberries, and the vintage, if not as pleasing as that from the apples had always proved, was good and she began to make a reputation for herself as a producer of consistent quality. But she could never make enough of it. No sooner was it ready than some occasion or another would have her sending someone to the big shed to carry back a few bottles. In recent times the reasons had been celebrations. There had been a couple of christenings: Oliver Francis Xavier and Denis Stanley Joseph Pius. In addition, Lucy Daisy Felicity Uí Carthaigh had bought a car with four doors, and news had come from Africa that the Jesuit missionary Albert Aidan Ledwidge had seen Kilimanjaro. All of these had placed a great strain on Bridget Gaynor's reserves, and it had become obvious to her that she would need to replenish them quickly if they were not to disappear altogether.

It was September and the day was a Wednesday. Bridget Gaynor was standing in her scullery washing out the demijohns in preparation for the making of elderberry wine. In the previous few days she had noticed that the good-natured absent-mindedness which had characterised Linus Gaynor's personality during recent months had become a more serious contemplative manner. She had also received word that he had made several astounding saves in a recent game, including a penalty. She had assumed that this marked the end of a period in her son's life when all seemed gay and without worry, to be succeeded by the realisation that marriage brings with it responsibility and commitment, and she was not displeased to have such a change take place for she felt it was time for him to come to such a conclusion. As she washed the demijohns in her scullery she heard a key turn in the front door, followed by Linus Gaynor calling her into the kitchen where he stood with Gretchen Murray. They told the old woman that they wished to be married and asked for her blessing.

Bridget Gaynor asked her son to leave her alone with Gretchen Murray for a few minutes. When he had gone, she embraced her and her eyes welled up with tears. They sat and drank tea, and as they did so Bridget Gaynor told the young woman that she must be absolutely certain of what she was doing. 'Thirty years may seem a long time,' she said to her, 'but when there are children about and you have little money it passes very quickly and before you know it your man is gone and you are left to fend for everyone.' Surviving without a husband had been done so many times before that everyone knew it was possible, but that did not mean that anyone found it easy. There were none of the women, except Fiona Sinead Deirdre whose husband had been a wife-beater, who would not have wished things to be different. This warning was a time-honoured ritual, but Bridget Gaynor detected no sign of any hesitancy in the young woman which would have given her cause to believe that the girl was temporarily blinded to reality. Nothing she could say to Gretchen Murray upset her in the least, and there was an air of expectancy about her which Bridget Gaynor thought almost fatalistic.

Linus Gaynor was called back into the room, and after a kiss from his mother and his wife to be he was dispatched to the big shed to bring back the last of the elderberry wine.

*

Having married each other, Linus and Gretchen Gaynor bought the house at the very edge of the town which had been built in the first decade of the century by Linus Gaynor's uncle Phillip Chester Eamonn. His uncle's widow had lived there for fifteen years on her own, but now she found that she could no longer fend for herself so she took a room at a nursing home in the capital where smiling men in nice suits charged her exorbitant fees to feed her a few times a day and provide her with new bedlinen once a month. Linus Gaynor took a job as a truck-driver, criss-crossing the country delivering window-frames to building sites. He no longer played between the goalposts, for time was money to him now and he took his responsibilities very seriously indeed. Linus and Gretchen Gaynor named the house Poule, after a small town where Gretchen had spent some time with an aunt a few years before which she spoke about with fondest memories.

Linus Gaynor returned to Poule every night, sometimes very late from the other side of the country, and he noticed a gradual change in the house. With every passing week it grew to be more comfortable. When they first moved into it, it bore all the signs of its most recent occupant. The walls were damp and the window-frames were rotting. There was also the musty smell of an unwashed human, as the widow of Phillip Chester Eamonn had been unable to clean herself properly for years. Despite the coats of fresh paint and the new timber that was used in the house, the smell lingered stubbornly. It seemed as intractable as the woodworm. But slowly, over a period of two years, Linus Gaynor found that he was less and less aware of the smell when he came back home at night. He was not sure if this was because he had grown accustomed to it or whether they had finally managed to eradicate it completely, so he invited Tomás Dent, the insurance representative who called every week, into the living-room to test a theory.

Tomás Dent was a tall thin man who wore thick glasses and a trilby hat and had upper dentures which roamed about his mouth like a predator, and in truth Linus Gaynor did not much like him. But he believed the insurance man was incapable of telling a lie, so for the first time in two years of business he invited him into the living-room. 'Tell me what you smell,' said Linus Gaynor to him.

The insurance man had been startled enough by the original invitation, and he was now completely thrown by the nature of what he was asked to do. He took several short snorts of air, twisting up his nose as he did so. He thought a little and then repeated the exercise. He was concerned not to upset Linus Gaynor, for clients were difficult to come by, so he answered that he could smell some very excellent cooking from the kitchen.

This was a complete lie, for there was nothing being prepared, so Linus Gaynor prompted him a little. 'You don't smell anything kind of dirty do you?'

'Oh heavens no!' grovelled Tomás Dent. 'Certainly not. Most definitely not.'

'You don't smell dirty flesh at all?' continued Linus Gaynor.

Tomás Dent was upset by this question, thinking that he might be in the company of a madman. 'Dirty flesh?' he whispered back to Linus Gaynor, then smiling nervously he shook his head from side to side. 'No, Sir – I can't say I do.'

Linus Gaynor thanked him for his honesty and then quickly showed him to the door. It did appear that they had managed to end the smell, and with it he felt that the house was now well and truly theirs.

Having children was always an urgency with the family. No sooner would the guests have been sent home from a wedding feast than the couple would begin consummation. Linus and Gretchen Gaynor were no exception, and within fifteen months of their marriage Gretchen gave birth to a boy which they agreed to name Darius, after Linus's father. To be exact, they named him Darius Edward Roger: Edward because they both thought it a handsome name and Roger after an uncle of Gretchen's who had died in some war or another.

Darius Edward Roger had been conceived to the strains of Benny Killeen's Dancehall Jazzband. The entertainer was making his first tour of the country since his release from prison, twenty years after his conviction for the murder of his trombone player while putting down a dressing-room coup. To many of his followers, Benny Killeen's actions were entirely forgivable and they maintained a nightly vigil outside his prison for several months after his conviction, playing jazz favourites on a gramophone to cheer him through his lonely nights. When he was finally released, his fingers no longer played piano with the same dexterity which had made him such a hero – this was due both to arthritis brought on by advancing years and to the limited amount of practice he could get in prison – but people came to see him in their thousands. For many the reason was nostalgia; for most, it must be said, it was simply curiosity about the man himself. Linus and Gretchen Gaynor were in this latter group. Like many others, they had been brought up hearing stories about the great Benny Killeen, and so when he came to the town they were there an hour before the doors opened at the Farmers' Hall.

It was true that Benny Killeen's fingers were not what they used to be, yet in a strange way this gave his playing an individual character. Benny Killeen's playing was not entirely correct but, like a retired tenor reaching for long forgotten notes, the inaccuracies imbued his tunes with an enchanting lilt. His lungs too were in bad repair, and his voice when singing trailed off more quickly than the composers had intended, but this again added to the mood of his performance and it took Linus and Gretchen Gaynor by surprise. They had gone there, as you go to a museum, intending to observe some old object. Yet what they found was something which moved them truly, and it was this effect which had Gretchen murmuring into her husband's ear. 'Take me to bed,' she whispered to him. 'We'll still be able to hear the music from there.'

It was an August night, and as they reeled and twisted on their bed they could clearly hear the sound of Benny Killeen's Dancehall Jazzband coming across the fields, through the new orchard of Grenadier apples and through the window, filling up the room. That was the night that Darius Edward Roger was conceived, in a passion which made the fading talent of an ageing musical master seem less forlorn. And although she cried in the immediate aftermath of their love, Gretchen Gaynor was never sure of the reason. 'One day one of us will die,' she said, 'but we will live for ever in heaven.'

Darius Gaynor was not to be an only child. In the succeeding years, Linus and Gretchen were to have another seven children: three boys and four girls. None of these was to be conceived in such memorable circumstances, indeed each successive pregnancy had less majestic beginnings, and it was on Darius Gaynor that most of the attention was centred. As he was the first child it was upon him that Linus and Gretchen Gaynor doted most fervently, believing that if he was to be successful in life he would prove an inspiration to his younger brothers and sisters.

As the boy grew and approached his teens, his father began to teach him all of the things he knew, and even many of the things he did not know. Linus Gaynor would closet young Darius in the shed at the bottom of the yard and try to show him how to be a carpenter, despite knowing nothing of the craft himself. They would spend hours there in the evenings, emerging well after dark with unstable chairs and rhomboid picture-frames. There were also lessons in how to cultivate plants. Consecutive springs in which endless rows of seeds were sown were followed by summers of barren harvests. Cabbages bolted as soon as they emerged from the soil, radishes fell prey to diseases specific to other crops, and turnips . . . well nothing was ever seen again of any of the seeds planted. These schoolings in carpentry and horticulture were repeated in other disciplines. Mechanics, mathematics, plumbing, even dentistry were all the subject of paternal tuition without any skills being transmitted, but none of this seemed to matter. It was only when he took the boy to the playing-fields that Linus Gaynor was able to speak with true authority, and there he did succeed in inculcating in his son the art of leaping and diving.

Throughout the years of his youth, Darius Gaynor proved an attentive pupil for his father. Only occasionally was the elder's knowledge tested by awkward questions from the boy: about why jars slid from the shelves he had erected, or why water gathered in the centre of the roof he had fitted to the tool-shed. To these questions Linus Gaynor was always able to manufacture a quick reply which seemed plausible if not studied in any depth. The boy had always accepted the reasons without query, believing the answers were furthering his knowledge. But as he became a young man, passing through his early and middle teens, the deficiencies of the teaching he had been given began to dawn on him. This was a very slow process. Initially he had not wanted to see his education as what it was, but, as time went by, certain inescapable facts became clear to him. The crooked shelves did not in fact compensate for the slanting ceiling, and multiplication was reversible. But no harm was done to the boy by these revelations of inadequacy: they happened at the right pace to allow him to take them in his stride, and there was never an instance when he felt betrayed. In fact they occurred at such a pace that their end result was to make him even more affectionate to his father, who, despite his dreadful teaching, had never denied the boy any of his time. No indeed, Darius Gaynor passed through his late teens with nothing but admiration for the effort which his father had put into caring for him, and that alone was sufficient for him to know that he was fortunate to have such a man as a father.

That was the way things were at Poule when Darius Gaynor was growing up. The absence of any war for the period of those twenty years (previously unheard of) meant that the economy of the country prospered. Along with so many others, Linus Gaynor was a beneficiary of that, and he spent all his working days driving the length of the country delivering this and collecting that.

By his mid-forties, Linus Gaynor was the elder statesman of his family. His older brother Peadar had died three years before in the same way that so many of the others had gone. Peadar Gaynor had never managed to become likeable, the morose gruffness of his earlier years remaining with him throughout, but he had nevertheless managed to marry, and when he went he left six children – all of them girls. This left Linus Gaynor the oldest male in the family, and it was to his authority that people turned during what they could only presume would be the few short years before he too went the traditional way. Despite what he knew was inevitable, he maintained an air of optimism, supported by Gretchen who recalled with increasing regularity the conversation she had had with Bridget Gaynor on the day of her engagement. The time did seem to have passed too quickly, but she comforted herself with the thought that the years had been good ones, just as she had predicted.

Gretchen Gaynor initially thought those years had come to an end on a morning in May when her daughter Elizabeth Ann Aoife left Poule to go to work in the apothecary which had opened in the town and which posed serious threats to the practitioners of witchcraft who had occupied a place of medicinal reverence for a thousand years. That the daughter of Linus Gaynor himself should take up employment in such a place was considered almost treacherous by those for whom the ancient traditions still held sway. But they were in the minority, and for most people the sight of so many potions and remedies on the shelves of the new establishment was a sign of hope for relief from the illnesses which had blighted their lives.

Elizabeth Ann Aoife was always second to leave Poule in the mornings. She did so an hour after her father had left to drive off down the country. This morning in May when she closed the door of the house and walked to the front gate she noticed that Linus's truck was still parked at the back of the yard where he always left it at night. She crossed over to it, and as she got nearer she noticed the figure of her father lying back in the front seat, his mouth open and his head bent to the side. Her screams brought the whole house out. Gretchen Gaynor had often wondered how her husband's demise would come about, and as soon as she heard the girl cry out she knew immediately that something had happened to him. She was the first to arrive at the door of the truck, and she opened it slowly lest he fall out, sending Elizabeth Ann Aoife away to fetch the doctor. Gretchen Gaynor climbed up beside her husband thinking only to hold his body for a few minutes, but as she did so she heard him breathe. In his eyes she saw the faint sign of life, and with that she yelled out to everyone to hurry, hurry, hurry. He was still alive.

When the doctor did arrive, on his big high nellie bicycle, he knew that there was little he could do. The pharmacist was also asked for an opinion, but he too was unable to help: there was nothing on his shelves which would alleviate the symptoms. So they loaded Linus Gaynor into the back of his truck, placing a mattress beneath him and blankets above him, and Darius drove them the twenty miles to the hospital where it was diagnosed that he had had a stroke and was as ill as he was fortunate. Linus Gaynor did not die, but he remained in a state of almost complete coma for several weeks. Many eminent physicians (or so they all referred to themselves) came to see him, but none of them could offer any hope of a cure. The length of their titles seemed to get longer, with each succeeding one that arrived, but even the one with the longest title of all could only carry out the cursory examinations which these men always do and then pronounce himself bemused at the patient's capacity for survival.

For several months Linus Gaynor remained in the hospital. Every day, and without fail, he received many visitors. His old truck was their mode of transport, leaving his home like a scheduled bus at the same time each day, sometimes carrying up to twenty people all dressed up in their herring-bone suits or cotton frocks and holding small gifts for the patient. Darius even went as far as to construct two wooden benches which he placed in the back of the truck, but both of these broke within three days and they were replaced by a length of carpet. When they reached the hospital, the visitors would form a procession leading up to where Linus Gaynor lay. There they would stand around his bed like a soccer team talking tactics. Occasionally one or more of them would come close to Linus's face and peer down into his eyes, which showed no signs of movement. When the nurse came around ringing the bell which tolled the end of visiting time, they would all kiss him in turn and proceed back to the truck, nodding and bobbing their heads at each other as they discussed the patient's condition.

So it continued for five months, during which there was never any slackening in the numbers of people who wished to go and visit Linus Gaynor despite the disruption which it caused to their lives.

After those five months, the doctors called Gretchen and Darius Gaynor together to tell them that there was nothing more they could do for Linus and that he would have to be removed from the hospital. The physicians said this with heavy heart, in full expectation that the news would come as a terrible blow to such a devoted family. But that was not the reaction they received. Instead, Gretchen Gaynor jumped from her chair and hugged her son and then both of the doctors. That she could take her husband home was a sign that he was now stable and in no imminent danger. She ran back to the ward to tell the fifteen or so people who were cluttered around his bed. They were all of the same opinion as her, though only after some prompting, but eventually they were all agreed that this was good news indeed and the doctors were greeted with a brief round of applause when they passed the ward door.

The following morning Darius Gaynor rose early to prepare the truck for the mission it had that day. Initially he had considered making a low bed which would fit neatly into the back, but, thinking of the fate of the two benches he'd made, he opted instead for a thick mattress placed on the floor beneath which he slung two ropes which would be used to tie Linus down. Beside the mattress, Darius placed an armchair for his mother to sit in and a basket of food was prepared in case they got hungry on the journey. Some of the women brought flowers, dahlias and lilac verbena, white baby's breath and love-in-a-mist were sorted into bouquets and hung on the sides of the truck to adorn it. At nine o'clock a small convoy left Poule. Led by Linus's truck, it included four other cars and a horse-drawn carriage, which would easily be able to keep up on the return journey as they would travel slowly for the patient's comfort.

When they reached the hospital, Linus was stretchered down the big marble staircase and into the yard. There he was lifted with infinite care into the truck and tied down with the ropes. Then the convoy set out again, its progress painfully slow, taking five hours to complete the journey on such bad roads. As it moved along, many of the travellers broke into communal prayer. At six o'clock they stopped to say the angelus, kneeling at the sides of the road as they gathered around the truck carrying Linus Gaynor. When they were not praying or talking among themselves, many of them were thinking of what an extraordinary thing this was. The old women in particular – those who had long since buried their husbands and who could remember that there was always an abundance of aged aunts but no uncles when they were young girls – were all thinking to themselves that this indeed was a special event and that for some reason Linus Gaynor had survived as none of the other men had done.

At Poule they had prepared his room for his return. When the truck arrived there were dozens there to greet him. They filled the garden of the house and spilled out into the dusty road. Linus Gaynor was lifted with care from the mattress on to a wooden stretcher which Darius had asked the carpenter Eamon Shand to build – it had handles for six bearers – and he began the last leg of his journey. They carried him through the crowd on their shoulders. It was a squeeze to get him through the door, but they managed. Up the stairs they took him and finally into his bedroom which over-looked the apple orchard. There they lay the stretcher on the floor and lifted him on to the bed. Gathered around him, the family was led in prayer by Father Timothy McKeown. This was, he told them, a cause for celebration, and they all nodded their heads in agree-ment. Then they left, except for Gretchen and Darius. They remained for a time, just sitting there beside the bed holding Linus Gaynor's hands.

It was autumn but still warm enough for the window to be opened. Gretchen told Linus Gaynor of the good crop there had been from the apple-trees that year. She had made a lot of wine with it. From where Darius sat he could see the playing-field where they had spent so much time jumping about with a football. Both Gretchen and her son could not but feel that the occasion was bitter-sweet. Neither said anything to the other, but later – much later – they would both confide what they were truly thinking that evening as they sat by the bed. It was true that Linus Gaynor was home. The much-loved man was back where he belonged, but what was there in the future for him? He had managed to break through the barrier which all of his male relatives had failed to do, but the injuries he had suffered were grave indeed. But for the time being they were not going to think about that. He was home at Poule where they could fend for him.

After half an hour they decided to leave him to rest. It had been a long day. Gretchen closed the windows and pulled the curtains. She switched off the light and blessed herself as she left the room.

Chapter Two

In the evening of the third Thursday in every month, a large white car would pass in front of Poule and park outside the American Hotel. From it would step the round figure of Judge Jervase Stearne, who always stayed at the hotel on the eve of his monthly judicial sessions in the town. Like so many of his predecessors, Judge Jervase Stearne was rarely sober. He was often seen slurping from a bottle of gin while driving, in broad daylight without making any attempt to conceal his actions, and he even continued to drink like this during cases he was hearing, often pointing the bottle at a participant as if it was his index finger. None of this had tended to enhance his reputation as a competent arbiter of the law, yet in a town without an alternative, whatever legal authority existed did so in the gin soaked figure of Judge Jervase Stearne.

On entering the American Hotel, the Judge would consume half a gill of gin before taking his seat in the restaurant. There he would be fed with numerous slices of bacon, several eggs, beans, tomatoes, mushrooms, chick-peas, celery and slices of turnover loaf. His conversation, if the term is not too inappropriate, was entirely functional during all of this: 'Give me this', 'Give me that', 'This is too cold', 'This is too salty',

'Where's my bill?' 'Where's my change?' With such an impoverished line in banter, the Judge could not be said to be a particularly popular figure, even though his behaviour had sometimes earned him a modicum of respect for its outrageousness. At the beginning of his thirty-year career on the bench, Judge Jervase Stearne had initially found it very difficult to convict anybody, even when the evidence was overwhelming. Indeed, even when defendants pleaded guilty the Judge would squirm about on his seat as he wondered what to do next. In such a court, guilt or innocence was immaterial as the penalties for the former were often indistinguishable from the rewards for the latter. But that was during the civil war, when judges were always under intimidation from the insurgents, and Judge Jervase Stearne's behaviour was seen by many as unquestionable evidence of a fellow-traveller in the rebel cause. This had lost him any chance of a place in the higher courts, and he was sent instead to preside over mundane cases in remote jurisdictions, administering justice in everything from a cattle showroom to a schoolhouse to a disused Presbyterian church.

The Judge had taken his demotion badly and his subsequent appearances were increasingly ill-tempered. There were times when he became so outraged at the indictments made against some defendants that he would climb over his bench to thump the man on trial and have to be physically restrained. In one celebrated case he had thrown his gavel at an impudent pork-belly smuggler, striking the accused above the left ear which caused blood to flow. But his anger had not always been directed at defendants. Some of his most bizarre outbursts had been against plaintiffs. He told a farmer who had clearly proved a charge of cattle-rustling against his neighbour that, because the accused had

31

fewer cattle than he, the court would dismiss the case. When the plaintiff protested, the Judge ordered him to hand over another Friesian for displaying such contempt for the law.

This had been the way of the Judge for the past fifteen years, during which time his increasingly erratic administering of justice had been accompanied by an indefatigable march towards obesity. Now when he sat in the restaurant of the American Hotel, the sweat teemed down his forehead and the sides of his face as he consumed huge amounts of food, and fellow diners were repelled by his body odour. After finishing his meal he would return to the bar and drink several pints of stout without any difficulty despite his full belly. He would speak only to order more liquor, but when he retired to his room the building would reverberate to his thunderous belches and the anguished screams of his bedsprings as he tossed and turned before falling asleep.

On rising in the morning the Judge would spend a few minutes at the wash-basin scrubbing beneath his armpits in a doomed attempt to exorcise the smell. Then he would fill his hair with macassar and comb it across so that not a square inch of his scalp could be seen above the parallel which he rigorously demarked half an inch above his thick eyebrows. He would then dress, take his wigbox in his hand and pull open the door as if expecting a large crowd to be gathered in waiting outside. Down in the grill he would consume another great meal before setting out for the stage of the Farmers' Hall which he used as his court. There he would be met by the Police Sergeant who would inform him of the day's cases. At one time the list to be heard would have meant a full day's work, but in more recent months there had been a significant diminution, often allowing the Judge to complete his business by midday.

On this particular day, Judge Jervase Stearne arrived at the Farmers' Hall to find the door locked. He circled the building several times, looking through any windows he could reach and banging on anything that resembled a door. But he could see no one, and no one came to answer his calls. After twenty minutes, the Police Sergeant arrived and informed him that there were no cases to be heard that day and apologised for wasting His Honour's time. Judge Stearne was filled with a mixture of relief and concern. He was relieved because it meant he did not have to preside over any boring cases that day, but he was also a little concerned, for this had never happened before and he thought it might indicate some disquiet at his competency. Trying to conceal his disquiet, the Judge walked past the policeman and squeezed himself into his car. Then he left the town, passing Poule as he did so.

Gretchen Gaynor would never forget the day it was discovered that her husband could not only hear what was being said to him but also possessed the ability to respond by blinking his eyelids. It was she who discovered it, two years after Linus Gaynor had been brought home, as she sat speaking to him without a scintilla of hope that he could hear. But she spoke to him anyway, as she did to her father at his grave. She sat on her big Hottentot's backside with her hands crossed on her lap and in her eyes she showed the patience of a lover deserted by everything but hope, recalling to the walls of the room the night she had cried after love because the day would come when one of them would die. 'This is not the kind of thing I had in mind,' she said. 'This is much worse. A real death is merciful sometimes, Linus. Like to the bull in the ring. But it seems you are to be toyed with for a while yet. Perhaps before you go you will waken for a minute, just for a minute, so I can tell you how much I missed you even though you were here all the time. Just for one minute, my dear. Wouldn't that be mighty?'

It was as she spoke the word 'mighty' that she looked at him and saw him blink once. It was not his blinking which made her think twice about what she had seen, for he did still blink, though with less regularity than before, but the timing of it seemed funny to her. So she repeated her question. 'Wouldn't that be mighty?' she said without taking her eyes off his, and he blinked once again. So she repeated the question a third time – 'Wouldn't that be mighty, Linus?' – and he blinked once again. Before she allowed herself to draw a defin- ite conclusion on what she was seeing, she made the sign of the cross and then knelt forward, resting her elbows on the bed beside her husband's shoulder and speaking as if she was in a confessional. 'Do you love me, Linus?' she asked him, and he blinked once again. So she paused while she gathered the confidence to ask a final question. After some seconds, during which the whole of their lives together passed before her, she asked him what she most wanted to know: 'Can you hear me, Linus?' He blinked once again, but this blink was followed by several more as tears formed in the corners of his eyes and ran down on to the pillow.

Gretchen Gaynor jumped to her feet and roared out the name of her eldest son who was sleeping down- stairs. 'Darius,' she screamed – 'Darius, come quickly. Dada can hear. He can hear.'

When he reached the room, Darius stood trembling at the foot of the bed, as much from the shock of such an awakening as from the things his mother was yelling. But he quickly joined her in a frenetic state and began himself to shout at his father. 'Dada, who am I,' he asked, but his mother interrupted.

'No, no, look at his eyes – his eyes. Ask him something and look at his eyes.'

So Darius ran up beside his father's head and bent down close to him. 'Dada, who am I?' he said.

'No, no,' yelled his mother. 'Out of the way. Let me do it.' And she pushed past her son and bent down close to her husband's head. She pointed behind her at her son, and the room went quiet as she calmed herself to ask the question. 'Is this your eldest son?' she said with the grit of a schoolmistress. Linus Gaynor blinked once, and she looked over her shoulder at Darius who nodded his head in acknowledgement that he had seen it.

'Dada,' said Darius moving closer to him, 'if you can hear me, blink once.' And his father did. 'And what if the answer is "no"?' said Darius, and his father blinked twice. ' "No" is twice,' said Darius, and Linus blinked once.

Darius Gaynor jumped to his feet and ran around the room as his mother went down on her knees for a last prayer. 'Sacred Heart of Jesus, thank you,' she said before joining her son jumping about the room and laughing like a pair of children.

It slowly emerged that Linus Gaynor was in full command of his mental faculties. Even with his limited vocabulary Linus Gaynor could take part in any conversation as long as everything was put to him in the form of a question. In this way he could comment on the weather, he could ask for more light, he could complain about his bedsores and ask to be turned on his side. All of this elevated the status of Gretchen

Gaynor, whose reputation rose by association, for she was the wife of Linus Gaynor – the man who should not have been alive. Now when she walked about the town her bearing defied her advancing years, and when people spoke to her they did so with an air of reverence, sometimes clasping their hands to their breasts revealing the humility they felt.

Two years after his return, the reputation of Linus Gaynor began to grow. Not only was he the most senior male in the family: that status was further enhanced by what had gradually come to be seen as a miraculous course of events. His room became the destination of many short journeys. When there was trouble in the family – poverty, sickness, bewilderment, crime – people often made the journey through the town to the gates of Poule. Up the garden they would go and in the front door. Mounting the stairs with Gretchen Gaynor, who would tap on the door before entering, they would stand – alone – at the foot of Linus Gaynor's bed with their hats in their hands and their heads bent low in deference. They would explain the reasons for their coming, sometimes going into long histories of the problem, and when they had finished they would leave. The next day they would return to ask what Linus Gaynor thought they should do. By the movement of his eyelids many problems had been solved, if not by the good sense of his replies then because the moral weight which his decisions began to carry was in itself enough to coerce disgruntled factions to cease their fighting and find more peaceful solutions.

The accounts of the events in Linus Gaynor's bedroom had not taken long to spread beyond his family. In the post office, in the church, in the covered market, in the funeral parlour, in all of these places and then in the open air itself, the story was that Linus Gaynor was indeed an excellent arbiter of disputes. This was why Judge Jervase Stearne had a decreasing number of cases to rule on, for the seat of justice had moved from the stage of the Farmers' Hall to the bedroom of Linus Gaynor, the room which the round Judge now drove past on his way back to the capital.

'Someday that old Judge will burst,' said Gretchen Gaynor to Alma Murnaghan as she led the young woman up the path to the front door of her house, up the stairs and into the room of Linus Gaynor. Alma Murnaghan had come to seek the counsel of the paralysed man on a matter of great personal concern to her. Like many others, she was drawn to see him not only by the reputation of the quality of the deliberations which issued from his room, which had spread out from Poule, but also by the complete confidentiality of the process. For no matter how much he might have wanted to speak to someone about the cases which came before him, Linus Gaynor had little means to do so, and so in addition to the cases to which secrecy was of no importance there came to him those problems which weighed heavily on people and which they had previously felt unable to speak to anyone about.

Alma Murnaghan had not been to see Linus Gaynor before, but the ritual had been explained to her by Meabh Slevin, who had become a pious devotee, not so much because she sought his advice but because her gannet's nose found the whole scene to be a fertile ocean for her Byzantine chatter. 'It's like standing in the court of a Patriarch,' she said to Alma Murnaghan. 'He has the presence of a generous dictator, and I swear that in the rhythm of his breathing I can sometimes hear the footsteps of the Blessed Virgin.' Gretchen Gaynor explained to the young woman how she must first outline the problem and then set out possible answers in a series of questions. After that she must leave and return the following day, by which time an answer would be ready. With that Gretchen Gaynor left the room, closing the door quietly behind her.

The room was hugely silent and all that could be heard was the slow breathing of the man in his bed. This might have been enough to scare Alma Murnaghan half out of her wits, but she was quickly aware of a real peace about the place which settled her, so she took a chair on the left-hand side of the bed adjacent to his head, coughed a little and began to speak.

What Alma Murnaghan had to say to Linus Gaynor was testament to the high esteem in which he was now regarded. Up to now, the issues on which his advice had been sought had been straightforward, and often boring. There had been disputes about land, cheating, bribery, overpricing. Advice had been sought about gambling on horses and on greyhounds. People had even come to him for guidance about their careers. Should they go to university? Should they become farmers? Should they follow their father's trade? Linus Gaynor had given an opinion on all of these issues, but they were what might be called honest topics. What Alma Murnaghan had to say to him that day was evidence that the scope of his influence was beginning to seep into a deeper level of the human condition.

Alma Murnaghan was now twenty five. She was plain in appearance, and nothing about her face or body had ever aroused great passion among men. But that was of no concern to her. For many years now, she had known privately, and without her ever telling anyone, that it was not to men that she was attracted. She told Linus Gaynor, whispering to him in case someone might be listening at the door, that as a young girl her eyes had strayed happily in the girls' changing-room after they played camogie in the sodden fields. It was absolutely out of the question that she should ever have tried to tell anyone about this, and even more impossible that she should ever have made advances at any of the other girls. For years she had hidden what she knew was natural to her. She had been courted by young men it was true, but nothing they had ever done or ever tried to do made her in the least attracted to them. In fact the more she was courted by them the more brutish she found them, but there was nothing she could do, lest her secret be revealed by the rumours of her abstinence. In the cause of protecting her love for women, she had endured many a cold hour in secluded places of fornication, and she had come to speak to Linus Gaynor because she could not stand her situation any longer. Should she marry a man, accepting the consequent sexual obligations during the years of childbirth, after which she would reject any further such activity in the privacy of marriage? Or should she leave and follow her natural instincts elsewhere, for she knew the town to be no place for a woman's woman to practise her ways?

When she had finished her story and posed her alternatives, Alma Murnaghan sat for a few minutes in the room without saying a word. She had all over her a feeling of ease that at last she had spoken to someone about what was, after all, her lifelong obsession. Even though she could receive no verbal reaction from Linus Gaynor, the fact that he was there and had not shown any shock at her story in some ways made her feel quite normal. She was happy with herself, and she even rested her hand on his arm for a moment before standing up to leave the room. At the bottom of the stairs she met Gretchen Gaynor, who wished her a good day and told her to return at the same time tomorrow.

Down through the town went Alma Murnaghan, extending greetings to everyone she met. A lot of them were surprised that the sometimes dour young woman was in such good spirits, yet they returned her greetings.

'Did you hear the Blessed Virgin?' enquired Meabh Slevin, who had been loitering among the exuberant confectionery in Maurice McKenna's expensive cake shop.

'I can't say I did,' replied Alma Murnaghan, 'but that is not to say that She did not hear me.'

That night as she lay in bed and thought to herself of what Linus Gaynor might recommend, Alma Murnaghan was still undecided about whether or not she would accept his deliberations without question. In fact, she thought that her adherence to his decisions would not be absolute but would depend on what he told her to do. She was sure of what she wanted him to suggest. If he advised her that she should follow her instincts and leave, then she would certainly do so, for it was what she wanted to do and all she needed was an encouraging opinion. But if he advised that she should stay and marry, then she was not at all certain that she could do such a thing. There was no one, not a single man that she had ever met, that she felt might make such a course bearable. No matter how considerate or generous he might be, Alma Murnaghan knew that there was not the man alive who could make her happy, and no amount of security and wealth could compensate her for living her life as such a protracted lie.

The following day Alma Murnaghan rose early and spent quite some time in her room applying make-up and combing her hair. When she had made herself as beautiful as she could, she ate alone in the kitchen. Then at the appointed time she set out for Poule, discovering as she walked the wide main street that she was praying to herself. This was the first time she had done so for many years, and she did not know what to make of the fact that it had started without her noticing. But there was no mistake about it: as she walked past the expensive cake shop of Maurice McKenna, she was suddenly aware that her lips were miming the words of the Memorare.

When Alma Murnaghan reached the gates of Poule, she found Gretchen Gaynor in the garden where she spent most of her mornings. Her constant attention had made the plants grow with such unbounded vigour that the hollyhocks were as high as the upstairs windows and strong enough to support the weight of a boy climbing on them. Alma Murnaghan was welcomed to the house and again taken up the stairs and into the room of Linus Gaynor, who lay exactly as he had done the previous day. She sat down near his head and, having reminded the young woman of the codes of his answers – one blink for 'Yes' and two for 'No' – Gretchen left them alone and returned to her flowers.

Alma Murnaghan asked Linus Gaynor if he thought she should stay and marry a man. He blinked twice. She asked him if she should leave. He blinked once. Then she asked if, when she did leave, she should follow her instincts and seek the company of other women. He blinked once again. She stood up and bent over to kiss his forehead, then Alma Murnaghan left the room and returned to the garden. There she embraced Gretchen Gaynor and told her of her admiration for her husband.

Within two weeks of her visiting Linus Gaynor, Alma Murnaghan had left the town. She did not give the real reason why she was doing so, preferring to say that there were better jobs elsewhere. When she had gone there was no one in the town except Linus Gaynor who knew of the secret she had concealed for so long. Every few months for the next couple of years a postcard would arrive at Poule addressed to Linus Gaynor from Alma Murnaghan. The postcards came from cities across Europe, and on them she expressed her enormous gratitude to him for his advice. But she never gave any hint of what that advice had been, and after two years the postcards stopped arriving.

Within three years of his arrival home, Linus Gaynor's jurisdiction was absolute – so much so that the round Judge Jervase Stearne stopped coming. After three more visits requiring no decisions from him he had given up, and his white car no longer groaned into the town on the third Thursday of every month. It would be correct to say that his absence was hardly noticed. It was not for months afterwards that Cearbhall MacGabhann happened to mention it during a deep conversation on the law which was taking place in The Kitchen. While outlining the details of an old bigamy case in which he had been forced to sit on the jury, he mentioned the fat judge. With that he stopped in mid sentence, reminding his fellow interlocutors that no sight had been seen of the man for quite some time. When they thought of it, they all had to agree with him and all surmised that the unnoticed absence of Judge Jervase Stearne was testament to the excellent nature of Linus Gaynor's law.

In the early months of the year there was not much for Gretchen Gaynor to occupy herself with. Her garden was dormant and the weather mostly too bad for her to spend much time out of doors, so she contented herself with making bread in the mornings and then in the afternoons sitting for two hours in the living-room, where she read thirty pages of a book. The winters at Poule always gave her plenty of time for thought, and it was during one of those occasions that she decided that the fifth anniversary of her husband's transformation should be marked in some way.

That afternoon she called the women together. Sipping tea, which some of them had laced with no small amount of whiskey, they discussed for hours how they could best remember that awesome day five years before. They first had to decide whether what they were remembering was a cause for celebration or a catastrophe, for despite all of the events of the previous five years, all of the problems which Linus Gaynor had solved and all of the people whose lives had been improved by his wisdom, no one was ever quite sure whether to speak of his condition as a blessing or a curse. Not even Gretchen Gaynor herself had answered that question, but it was Dearvla Deirdre Concepta who seemed to be clearest in her mind that the anniversary should indeed be a celebration. 'Look at the rest of us, honey,' she said to Gretchen Gaynor. 'At least you can speak to your husband every day and touch him and care for him. But look at the rest of us. We're all just old relics waiting for we don't know what. When we have anniversaries for our men we always wear black. Everyone comes and commiserates with us and we sit around in a circle eating lettuce and wishing that whoever it is we are remembering was still with us. How can we think of comparing Linus Gaynor's anniversary with such events? It seems to me that this must be a cause for celebration. I think that it should even be a party, though I mean no disrespect.'

The more they spoke of the event, the stronger the case for celebration became. Although she did not indulge in any of the whiskey, Gretchen Gaynor gradually became delighted with her decision to mark the event, the enthusiasm of her friends providing her with the inspiration she needed. That evening she donned her best flowery dress, which was inconsistent with the weather but in tune with her mood, put on her big red coat with the fake white fur collar and set out for the house of enormous Father Raymond Curtis.

The study, if so it could be called, had barely grown beyond the eighteen books which the room had housed on the evening that Bridget Gaynor had sat in the dishevelled armchair by the window and first enquired about the name of the second Pope. The books had been shifted around and regrouped during various alterations to the décor of the room, but their number remained small and their pages had seldom been opened. Father Raymond Curtis was an enormous man. Even by the standards of big men, he was enormous. In his earlier years he had been a dangerous rugby lock forward, and he continued to play after his ordination. Beneath the smouldering mounds of scrummaging bodies, the ferocious tongue of Father Raymond Curtis could always be heard bellowing obscenities at his playing partners, and his name was a constant entry in referees' notebooks, for referees were often the targets of his filthy mouth. Yet when he changed into his clerical black he was a different man. His manner was always courteous, and Gretchen Gaynor was received with great civility when she knocked on his door. She was led into the study and seated in the big armchair by the window and there she outlined her plans to celebrate the forthcoming anniversary of her husband's blessed stroke with a mass and a party.

The priest was delighted with the woman's courage in accepting her lot. 'You might even consider a rugby match as part of the occasion,' he suggested. But this she declined, thinking it too physical a game for such an occasion. The priest agreed instantly and apologised for any offence he might have caused.

When she returned home that evening, Gretchen Gaynor took her notebook from behind the clock on the living-room mantelpiece and set to work making lists. She was forever making lists. She could not undertake any job without first making a list about it. Her pockets were always full of slips of paper containing lists of objects, people, things to do, things to get, things to lift, days to remember. Every facet of her life was contained on a list and quite often on several lists. That night she made out more of them, and her husband had long since fallen asleep by the time she went to kiss him goodnight.

His frequent forays from the town to watch rugby games and the height at which he towered over everyone else had not prevented Father Raymond Curtis realising the esteem in which Linus Gaynor was held by the people. The priest had often been asked to celebrate mass in houses. The requests had always been granted and he would arrive at the appointed address with all his instruments of the ceremony and robe himself in a private room set aside. But that would not be appropriate in this instance. For this was no ordinary mass: this was for Linus Gaynor. On the day in May which held the anniversary, a large crowd gathered outside the presbytery in the early afternoon. They were all dressed to match the importance of the occasion. There were many fine suits and polished boots. Frocks and stilettos were much in evidence, as were greasy heads of well-oiled hair. When he was ready, Father Raymond Curtis nodded to one of his altar boys to open the front door of the presbytery. The crowd fell silent as he came out through the gate, turned left and led the procession along the dusty road in the direction of Poule. As they went they sang hymns and said a decade of the rosary, and there was much beating of breasts and bowing of heads.

When they reached the house, the priest walked up the path to the opened front door, climbed the stairs and stood at the top, opposite the room where Linus Gaynor lay. All the time he was murmuring to himself, though even his murmur was a loud hum. Then bending down so as not to decapitate himself with the lintel, he entered the bedroom. He found a small altar erected at the foot of the bed at which he could stand. Towering above Linus Gaynor Father Raymond Curtis blessed himself with a wide sweep of his right arm, and his booming voice travelled out the window, through the walls to wherever the crowd had settled. There was no need for amplification of the voice of Father Raymond Curtis. Even those who knelt in the dust and on the grass outside could clearly hear every word he said, and loud responses rose up to his prompting. On some occasions the crowd began to sing, filling the air with uncanny harmonies before falling silent again in waiting for the big voice in the house. And all down the stairs knelt the tribe of old women who had buried their husbands, all of them wearing their black mantillas and twisting beads in their hands, thumping their chests and whispering sibilant adorations to themselves.

When the mass was finished, Father Raymond Curtis blessed Linus Gaynor and spoke of his admiration for the courage with which the man had faced such a cataclysmic change in his fortunes. 'There are those among you – many among you,' he said – 'who believe that in his very being here with us, Linus Gaynor is in some way a gift from God. Looking at him here I cannot disagree with that. He is indeed a wonder, and we all have much to be thankful for.' With that the priest concluded his task and put away his robes and artefacts. The crowd broke up into small groups, and from some of them came the beginnings of song. Gretchen Gaynor began to direct people to the food on the tables in the kitchen, though many had already indulged themselves. She then sent Ronan Tiernan Hugh and Eoin Stafford Aidan to the shed at the bottom of the yard with instructions to bring back all of the apple wine that was there.

Gretchen Gaynor's wine did not last long that evening, but that did not matter, for when it was finished people went to the pubs and brought back beer. There was music from Milo Bermingham, who had come with three of his brothers. He was not a particularly good violinist, but he believed his playing to have veterinary qualities. In the spring he would play to the ewes in the fields, and he had no hesitation in stating that the pleasant melodies soothed the animals' labours and reduced the number of stillbirths among the lambs. Along with his brothers Ivor, who was not a very good banjo player, Ignatius who was terrible on the tin whistle, and Mervyn who knew only one tempo on the bodhran, he managed to keep people dancing. Those who did not dance, or who could do so no more, sat on the ground and ate pieces of bread and meat they had stuffed in their pockets before the mass had even begun. There were lovers too – quite a few of them, for the town was never short of lovers. On the manicured grass which Gretchen Gaynor had that afternoon cut for the first time since the winter, they lay oblivious to

the damp, and when they had done all that was possible in public some of them left for more solitary places.
Over the ditches, in the sheds, behind the doors of cars,
beneath the privet hedges, in all of these places there
was kissing and tumbling.

While all of this was going on, the room where Linus
Gaynor lay was dark even though the curtains were
open. There was no one in the room with him. No one
had come to see him for over an hour, for they believed
that by now he would have been exhausted by the
events of the day and would wish to sleep. It was true
that listening to the booming voice of Father Raymond
Curtis did make a person tired, and the priest's
speeches had often engendered the most pernicious
migraine, but Linus Gaynor did not have a headache.
Whether his stroke had rendered him incapable of
having one he did not know, but he did not have one
and neither was he tired. In the darkened room, where
the smell of the new-mown grass cut through the body
odour and perfume which still hung about, in among
all those smells Linus Gaynor lay in the dark. Through
the window he could hear the awful tunes of the
Bermingham brothers and the off-key singing which
accompanied it. He could hear the giggling of the
young lovers from wherever they lay. What he was
thinking no one knew, but he lay motionless as he had
done for five years, and down the sides of his face and
into his ears ran the trails of tears, gathering on his
pillow in two damp patches, washing down from his
head whatever it was that had made him cry, carrying
away the thoughts which had upset him as he had not
been upset since he had found his cat dead in a rabbit
trap. Not since then, a time when Linus Gaynor was
nine years of age, not since that day in what he thought
must have been early autumn, maybe the beginning of

September, not since then had Linus Gaynor cried with such earnestness as he now did. There was no one there to witness it and perhaps that was fortunate, for people did not think of Linus Gaynor as being one for crying. The majestic figure from whom they derived such judicious counsel, the urbane cadaver himself could surely not be bothered with mere tears. But there he was indeed, like nothing anyone had ever thought he could be, with water streaming from his eyes but his chest absolutely still. With not a sound to be heard. Not an iota.

By the following morning nothing was left as evidence that Linus Gaynor had cried. The pillow was dry, as were the sides of his face and his ears, and when Gretchen Gaynor came to open the window and freshen the room she spoke with great satisfaction of the day they had had. All through the morning people called to make that very point. 'What a wonderful ceremony,' said Betsy Farquharson. 'I was very moved I was.' 'Never the likes of it before,' said Mona Dack as she helped herself to yet another cup of tea. What most of them were trying to say but lacked the courage to do so was that throughout the whole affair they had felt a certain spirituality which seemed to penetrate the walls of Linus Gaynor's bedroom and diffuse among them. Something seemed to be leaving the room where the man lay as the big priest went through his prayers. Milo Bermingham could vouch for that. He came with his brother Donncha as he was missing the dirty handkerchief which he always placed under his chin when he played violin. 'It's true what people are saying to you, Gretchen,' he said. 'I could sense it and I was standing quite far back.' The two brothers spent an hour in the garden looking for the rag, pulling up seedlings in the mistaken impression that they were clearing weeds. By late evening, Gretchen Gaynor was able to tell her husband that there had been such a warm response to the day. 'Everyone says so,' she assured him. But the man never acknowledged what she said. He didn't even blink an eyelid.

For Darius Gaynor, perhaps the only positive outcome of his father's paralysis was that he had inherited his truck. In the years before he collapsed behind its wheel, Linus Gaynor had come to love his truck. During his long excursions into unknown countryside he was never short of words for the vehicle and he spoke to it as if it was an animate companion. Now that Linus Gaynor would no more go driving in it, his eldest son took it upon himself not only to carry on his father's business but also to care for the truck. It came to receive the most tender devotion that any machine could expect. Darius Gaynor's legs could regularly be seen sticking out from beneath the vehicle in the evenings as he searched for what he thought might be the signs of fatigue. He polished the leather seats in the cab so much that his backside skidded across them as he travelled the winding roads and only his grip on the steering-wheel prevented his disappearing out the doors. He anointed the dashboard with fragrances pilfered from his mother's dressing-table and rubbed the leaves of lemon balm on the steering-wheel so that his hands smelt of citrus.

In the four years since he had commenced business, Darius Gaynor had built up a successful trade. To new contacts, he always introduced himself as 'Darius Gaynor, son of Linus'. He even had this printed on the invoices which he was sometimes asked to provide (although almost everything he did was for cash). How much this had to do with the success he enjoyed was difficult to say, but it was probably a combination of the name and his own acumen which allowed him to return home in the evenings with his pocket full of banknotes. With this money, Darius Gaynor was able to provide a comfortable living for those who remained at Poule. With it too he was able to buy the best treatments for his father: oils which he would heat and rub into the old man's joints to prevent arthritis, and expensive creams to smear on his bedsores to stop them becoming infected. These tasks Darius Gaynor performed without complaint, and his loyalty was often noted by those who came to the house.

At the hour of the morning when Darius Gaynor would set out on his day's journey, there would never be a soul to be seen. It was so early that even the cockerels looked tired and staggered about the yards in a half daze. Darius Gaynor had no reservations about rising at such an early hour, and it was always a source of satisfaction to him that by the time most people were climbing from their beds he had already worked for two hours. One morning in June he climbed into his gleaming truck and left Poule on his way to pick up a consignment of Howgate Wonders which had to be taken to the port. Leaving the town, he was alone on the road but there was nothing unusual about that. The edge of the town was marked by the house of Milo Bermingham, who lived there with two of his brothers, Leo and Fergus. As he passed the silent house, Darius noticed a small black car travelling towards him. It passed him some moments later and he could see two men sitting in the front seats, neither of whom he recognised and neither of whom made any gesture of acknowledgement to him. He did not think too much of this, except for his slight surprise at having to share the road at such an early hour of the day. The car continued into the town, where it stopped outside the American Hotel. The two men got out and went to the door of the building, but despite some persistent knocking no one came to open it, so they returned to their car and sat without speaking for another hour.

It was to be Benedict Quigley who spoke to them first. He was making his way to the American Hotel, where he was employed in the kitchens as a food slicer. His skill was his ability to halve everything again, no matter how thinly it had previously been cut. Using nothing more than a sharp knife, he spent his mornings meticulously recutting rashers into even thinner slices. Bread suffered the same treatment, as did tomatoes, tripe, black pudding, liver, kidneys and mushrooms. He even insisted that eggs be overfried so that he could slice one egg into two roundels. But before he got to the door of the American Hotel that morning, Benedict Quigley was accosted by the two men from the black car. He said that they sat and watched him walk nearer and nearer, never taking their eyes off him. When he was twenty yards away they simultaneously opened the doors of the car and got out, standing together on the footpath until he reached them. He was convinced he was about to be set upon, and at such an early hour there would be no one around to rescue him. Before either of them spoke to him, he was already insisting that he had no money in his pockets as his payment from the hotel was so miserly, despite the money he saved it through his craft of slicing. But the men were not interested in robbing Benedict Quigley; they simply asked him to point out the house of Linus Gaynor and let him go on his way once he had done so.

For the next few hours, the two men stood opposite the house of Linus Gaynor, one of them staring continuously at the building and muttering words out of

the side of his mouth to the other who wrote everything down in a pink-covered notebook. Úna Cribben
watched them the whole time they were there. She
could see them clearly from her bedroom window
where she sat for the entire morning darning her sons'
ferociously smelly socks. This she had to do with cotton
wool inserted in both her nostrils lest she forget to
breathe through her mouth and inhale the noxious
odour to which she attributed the death of her beloved
Dublin Bay rose which had once graced the walls near
the clothes line. 'They spent over two hours there,' she
said. 'I think they were taking notes of all of the
comings and goings, for the tall one who did all the
talking increased the speed of his mouth whenever
anyone arrived or left.' Jody Harcourt spent the morning looking at them too. 'I couldn't help it,' he said;
'they were standing right outside my window. All I
could see were two large backsides.'

When they had finished observing Poule, the two
men went back into the town, and it was there that they
introduced themselves as officials from the Ministry of
Justice. They spent the afternoon in the American Hotel
fishing for pieces of information about the things which
happened in the house. They were anxious to speak to
anyone who had been there, especially when Linus
Gaynor was presiding on a case. But they found people
unwilling to speak, for they had never been respecters
of officialdom. Only Barney Allott spoke to them in the
detail they were interested in. This was both because he
was flattered that someone should display such an
interest in him, especially someone in possession of an
identity card, but more particularly because he spent
the afternoon being filled with whiskey, which no one
doubted was at the taxpayers' expense. This latter
attraction outweighed all the attempts made to prize

him away from the men. Telephone calls were made to summon him from the bar, but each time he returned to finish his whiskey. Leo Bermingham sent his sister with orders to pretend to be Barney Allott's wife. She was to stand at the door and shout at him, then cross the room, take hold of his ear and pull him out. But she could not go through with it. Her nerve disintegrated after her first yelp and she ran back into the street, where Leo Bermingham cursed her ancestors. In all the two men from the Ministry of Justice spent three hours with Barney Allott, filling an entire notebook and half a second one. When they had gathered all that they needed, they put enough money behind the bar for their informant to have several more whiskeys, but once they were gone Barney Allott was barred for life and forever carried the indelible stigma of a tout.

When he arrived home that night, Darius Gaynor found his mother in a state of anxiety. She had spent the whole day wondering what the two men were up to. She met Darius at the door and told him that she feared something terrible was going to happen. 'They're going to take him away,' she said, 'I know something is going to happen. We must protect him. We must organise ourselves. We'll have to watch over him twenty-four hours a day. I know people will help. We can draw up a rota so that he's never alone.'

It took Darius some minutes to calm his mother. There was nothing to be concerned about he reassured her. There was no reason in the world why anyone should want to take Linus Gaynor away. 'How can a man like him be guilty of anything. He can't even go to the toilet by himself, so how could he be accused of a crime?'

During the succeeding weeks nothing more was heard of the visit of the two officials from the Ministry of Justice and the only evidence of their presence was the continuing ostracisation of Barney Allott, who hollered through the windows of the American Hotel that he was still owed several whiskeys. It was not for another two months that the town received the first repercussions of the day the civil servants paid their visit. The news came by way of the Police Sergeant, Donald Kilgallon, who arrived in the American Hotel one day and announced that they were sending a new judge. 'What do they want to do a thing like that for?' said Milo Bermingham, who was so bemused that he interrupted a lament on his violin. 'We have no need for a judge here any more. Surely they can see that.'

The news about the new judge was broken to Linus Gaynor by his wife. She had heard it from Meabh Slevin, who shouted it to her through the window as she ran by on the way to have another ridiculous perm inserted in her hair. Gretchen Gaynor went into Linus's room and stood like a scolded child at the foot of his bed. There she spoke apologetically of the news she had heard, but the old man made no response of any significance. He seemed neither upset nor impressed.

The following Thursday, at half past nine in the morning, a blue car pulled up outside the American Hotel. From it stepped a small thin man with suspect black hair and black patent shoes which were conspicuously polished. He walked to the police station, where he surprised Police Sergeant Donald Kilgallon who was scratching his scrotum through his trousers and letting out a sigh of relief as he did so. Turning around and picking a morsel of bacon from between his teeth with the same hand which had untangled his genitals, the Sergeant let out a second grunt, this time of surprise as he observed the stranger standing at the door of his untidy office. 'Good morning,' said the thin man. 'You must be Police Sergeant Donald Kilgallon.'

'That's correct,' replied the officer of the law, straightening himself a little in appreciation of the three stripes on his sleeve having been observed. 'And who are you?'

'My name is Olin Prescott. I'm the new judge.'

No sooner had the thin man spoken these words than the officer began convulsively to tidy his desk, straightening all of the scattered pieces of paper into arbitrary piles, emptying the ashtray into an imaginary bin on the floor behind him, and draining a cup of tea he had made himself an hour before.

'You have let people know I was coming today I presume,' said the Judge.

'Oh yes indeed, Your Honour,' replied the officer. 'Let me escort you to the hall.'

As the men crossed the street they exchanged only terse observations about the weather. Their passage was not unnoticed and there were many people who looked at Donald Kilgallon in a way which enquired if the man beside him was the new Judge. His grimaced face gave them the answer they looked for: this was the man. 'They don't make them like they used to, do they?' said Ignatius Bermingham to his dog. 'The last one was a fat slob, but look at this one. There wouldn't be much chewing on his bones.'

The Police Sergeant unlocked the doors of the Farmers' Hall and helped the Judge set up a table on the stage. With a handkerchief he found in his pocket, the officer cleaned the seat of a wooden chair and placed it behind the table. With that the Judge told him he could leave if he wished. It was more from embarrassment than obedience that the officer did so, for he knew in his soul of souls that no one would come to the court that day. It was not that people were unaware that the court was in session – nothing had stimulated more conversation in the previous weeks than the arrival of the new Judge – but he knew that no one would take advantage of it, for the formal channels of justice had now been disregarded for years. By way of consolation for this, the Police Sergeant spent much of the morning carrying cups of putrid tea across to Judge Olin Prescott, each time unconvincingly feigning surprise that no one had turned up.

In truth, Police Sergeant Donald Kilgallon had no need to act surprised at the non-existent turnout, for the Judge himself had not expected anyone to come. The reason for his visit that morning was to see for himself the place described in the report which the two civil servants from the Ministry of Justice had compiled from their notes. Judge Olin Prescott was no fool and he had bothered to come at all only to signal his intent. He took no pleasure from the unaccompanied hours he spent sitting behind the wooden table on the stage of the Farmers' Hall, but he did not consider it a waste of time either, for he had brought plenty of documents with him which required work. These received his mental attention, while his physical presence, albeit a spare one, was intended to signal that the rule of proper law would again be restored to the town.

At one o'clock in the afternoon the Judge packed his documents into his leather case and crossed to the police station. The building was locked, so the Judge took a slip of paper from his case and wrote a note on it. He thanked the Sergeant for his assistance and asked that he let the people know that the court would sit again in two weeks. He slipped the note beneath the door and walked to his car.

There were many people who watched the Judge's blue car drive through the town and out into the countryside. As he passed them, they looked at him without any signs of emotion, nor did they make any gestures of deference. He was neither surprised nor annoyed by this. Although a man in his position was used to being treated with respect, he knew from the civil servants' report that anything short of actual violence against him would be a small victory. So as he drove away he occasionally watched them looking back, quietly pleased with his work that morning and thinking to himself that the long process of recovering the town for the law had begun satisfactorily.

But that was not how the people of the town felt. No sooner had his car disappeared from view than loud shouts could be heard. In the bar of the American Hotel, where a number of men had gathered, the Judge's exit was greeted with an immediate rush to have someone buy a round. The Police Sergeant was with them but refused to volunteer. Gretchen Gaynor also watched the Judge's car leave. She was standing in her garden in the company of the failed actress Dorothy O'Leary, pretending to mulch her herbaceous border, when the blue car drove past at a very respectable speed. From between the awakening day lilies she peered out with a smile on her face and accepted the congratulations of her fellow worker, who patted her on the back and reminded her of how upset she had been when she first heard news of the new Judge. 'That's the end of him,' nodded Dorothy O'Leary, 'he didn't last long, did he?' Her sentiments were repeated by Darius Gaynor when he returned home in the evening and spoke to his mother in mocking self-congratulation of how he had been sure all along that nothing would come of this Judge and that Linus Gaynor's place of honour was under no threat.

That feeling of having seen off the Judge continued for the whole evening and into the night. The only one who could have stopped it was the Police Sergeant, but he was too intoxicated to read the note when he returned and instead went to bed, where he fell asleep fully clothed. It was not until the following morning that the truth became known. The note on the floor was the first thing Donald Kilgallon saw when he came out of his bedroom. It spoilt his day before it had even begun. He uttered a number of venial curses, for he knew he would be dragged like a hostage into any confrontation between the people and the Judge. Despite having one of the easiest positions in policedom, he sympathised with himself for the quandary he could sense building up around him. His self-condolence complete, he ate five rashers and went to tell the others.

Chapter Three

Darius Gaynor was now twenty-six years of age. His unquestioning devotion to his father had won him many admirers, and his name had become a byword for loyalty throughout the town. Everyone was impressed that such a man – for a man he had become – could spend so much of his time furthering the happiness of someone else, oblivious, or so it appeared, to his own self-interest. But that was indeed the way it appeared to be. To make any remark to Darius that touched on this loyalty was only to elicit an embarrassed dismissal of it, a consummate exhibition of modesty without parallel. In the mind of this young man there seemed no more important objective than to perform for Linus Gaynor those things which he could no longer do for himself and, in so doing, to ensure that Linus could continue to occupy the position he now held. There was no question in Darius's mind that, in doing the things he did, he was feeding the perpetuation of hope which was embodied in his father's ability to live on when he should not have been able to do so. Darius Gaynor's intentions towards his father were entirely altruistic and no premeditated schemes fuelled his generosity. What was not true about the image he portrayed was that he had neglected his own well-being entirely.

The first time he had seen Roberta Staunton had
been totally unmemorable. Looking back, he was not
surprised that the woman he now loved had made no
immediate impression on him – that their first
encounter had set no bells ringing in his ears such as
greeted the first meetings of the lovestruck characters
in the animated cartoons he saw in the Colisseum
Picture House. In the adolescent dreams of how he
might react when he first saw the woman he would
eventually marry, he had always thought that the occasion would pass unnoticed. His belief was that such a
beginning would augur far better for the longevity of
the affair than anything more dramatic. Love at first
sight was all very well. It was what most people wished
for, but for Darius Gaynor such an initiation could
never be sustained. From the very outset a romance
suffused with such immediate passion was as flippant
as a beautiful whore, because it gave up all its secrets in
an instant. And the first encounter between Darius
Gaynor and Roberta Staunton had indeed passed without either of them noticing, so now when they spoke
about it they could only speculate on when it had
occurred. How it had happened was not a problem; the
question was when. All they could be sure of was that
they had known each other for two years, three months
and an additional length of time which they guessed
must have been two or three weeks.

The circumstances of the first meeting they could
recall were concerned with the details of paperwork, or
rather the absence of details of paperwork, submitted
by Darius Gaynor when he made his twice-weekly
delivery of sultanas and ginger to the Worthy Bakery. It
was there that Roberta Staunton worked, and her
attempts to do so efficiently were constantly frustrated
by the inadequate paperwork handed in by the drivers

who delivered the ingredients for the bakery's products. Their invoices were always dated wrongly if at all, incorrectly totalled or without order numbers. This drove the young woman quite mad, less because she had to spend time correcting the invoices than because her persistent appeals to the drivers to improve the situation were almost completely ignored. Darius Gaynor was no different to so many others. Lemon Hands, as he had become known to the women in the clerk's office, was as guilty as the next, and no amount of badgering from Roberta Staunton's superiors had made any impression on him. On a particular day in September, Lemon Hands was confronted by the young woman from the clerk's office in a manner which at the time caused him no small amount of embarrassment. In front of a number of his fellow drivers he received a thundering rebuke from Roberta Staunton, who had been given an invoice by him just as her temper needed only one last push to send her into a rage. Before he drove out of the bakery yard, she ran from the office and spent several minutes yelling at him without giving him a chance to defend himself. 'What's the matter with your brain?' she roared at him. 'Is there anything between your ears that works? I'm sick to the teeth of telling you about your paperwork. You wouldn't get money out of heaven with an invoice like this.' When she had vented her spleen, there was nothing he could do but climb into his cab without any dignity whatsoever and drive off until he found a spot where he could sit and lick his wounds.

That was their first conversation, if that is the right word, which they could put a date to, for the date at least had been written on the invoice that Lemon Hands had given her. In view of what was to happen to them in the future, it was fortunate that neither of them was inclined to bear a grudge, for within weeks of that scene in the yard they were conversing like long-time friends on the occasions when Darius Gaynor would deliver his invoices and point out in minute detail that there were no incorrect or absent statistics on them.

The step which took them from a casual joviality inspired by paperwork to walking hand in hand along the quays near the Worthy Bakery took no more than a fleeting invitation from Darius Gaynor. Up until the moment he suggested that they spend a lunch together, they had never spoken of anything which was not in some way related to the delivery of sultanas and ginger. In the days before he transformed the nature of their conversation with his unsolicited invitation, he had wondered to himself – and being a truckdriver he had plenty of time to wonder – what opinions Roberta Staunton had about all of the other objects and pursuits of life. He had wondered if she was in any way interested in sport, if she was a good cook, how she dressed when she was not working, what sort of pet names she had for her mother and father. Darius Gaynor had no idea of the answers to these questions, and it was as much his desire to discover such details as it was his burgeoning affection for the young woman which made him interrupt a routine moment of banter regarding a consignment of ginger with an open invitation to walk with him along the quays for an hour. 'Will you take a walk with me at midday?' he asked her. 'You can look upon it as a reward for my clerical efforts.' She was as nervous as he and gave a very rapid answer of 'All right,' allowing them both to return to the safer ground of jokes about form-filling before any blushes had the chance to emerge.

The first day that they walked along the quays as petrified sweethearts was to be the beginning of an affair which for quite some time existed only in the hours around midday, seeming to be sustained by the warm sunlight of that time of day and the sound of the wash from the steamers breaking against the concrete piers. For reasons which neither of them spoke about to the other, they were both content to limit their court-ship to those hours. This atmosphere of restraint from prying too deeply into the other's private life was a consensus affair, and both seemed happy that it should remain that way for some time. For Darius Gaynor it meant that he could only go so far in gaining answers to the questions he had wished to ask, for Roberta Staun-ton would dismiss any questions which went beyond his allowed limits of investigation with 'Let's talk about something else,' and a forced laugh. He immediately understood, for he too was guilty of concealing things which they might have talked about. Most notably, he never told her about his father and how he now lived, lying in a bed year after year when everyone be-lieved his time had come a long while ago. Darius Gaynor thought that to recount this would in some way frighten the woman, as he had often noticed children being frightened by the spectacle of Linus Gaynor's motionless body when they were taken by their mothers to pray by his bed. He believed that unless you had known Linus Gaynor when he was able-bodied, unless you had seen how high he could leap and had been spellbound by his conversation, unless you had witnessed all of those things yourself, then the idea of him as he now was could only be a chilling vision of decay. For this reason, Darius Gaynor would make only casual reference to his father, and he was convinced that she suspected nothing unusual from his tone.

This was the manner of their affair for a number of months. They would walk for half an hour then sit where the whiskey ships moored and eat their bread and meat. Then they would walk back, stopping before they were visible from the Worthy Bakery to exchange the most chaste of kisses. It was always placed with infinite silence on each other's lips, so exquisitely that the lips were never bent out of shape. During these petite exchanges Darius Gaynor would close his eyes, as he felt it ungentlemanly to stare at a woman as she kissed him. But on opening his eyes again he would always see that hers were open already, and once they saw each other seeing each other their heads would draw back to formally end that part of the day. When he had seen her back to the yard of the Worthy Bakery and they had said their goodbyes, he would drive away with the promise that he would return in a few days.

It is possible that they could have continued in such a way for years. Neither ever displayed a desire to graduate to anything more intimate, but after three months of midday affairs Darius Gaynor did wish that he could have one truly long lip-bending kiss from Roberta Staunton. The day he chose to fulfil his wish was a Friday. He felt that Friday was always an auspicious day, for they both would be looking forward to a rest from the toils of the week. They walked as usual to the whiskey ships and ate. Then they returned to the spot which had become synonymous with exquisite courtship. They projected their heads until their lips touched and then Darius Gaynor wrapped his arms around her back and pulled her close to him. There was nothing the woman could do. It was not that she struggled to get free, but when he thought he was about halfway through he opened one of his eyes slightly, hoping to see her eyelids firmly shut in enjoyment. Instead she was staring at him from such a close range that he immediately became self-conscious about what he was doing and had to stop. He coughed more vigorously than was usual and placed his right hand over his mouth as if to hide an offensive weapon.

When he drove away that day he was furious with himself, for though she had said nothing by way of admonishment to him for his sexual bravado, he had seen for himself that his best efforts at kissing had failed to close her eyes. This was a cause of frustration to him. Up to that day her behaviour had been understandable. There was nothing very arousing in the timid exchanges which had marked the ends of their midday trysts, and he could understand that she would find no compelling need to concentrate in darkness during those brief moments. But this time he had done his best. He had contorted his face and she had seen it all from a very close range. 'That was no good,' he thought to himself – his impatience had got him nowhere.

What Darius Gaynor was not to know as he drove away from the Worthy Bakery that day was that the damage he had inflicted was more serious than he imagined. It was true that Roberta Staunton had seen his face screwed up and that it was not a particularly attractive sight, but that was not why she refused to see him on the following Tuesday when he came for lunch armed with a turnover loaf, five slices of spiced beef and an apology. 'She left half an hour ago,' said one of her assistants, 'and she'll not be back before three this afternoon. She gave me this for you' – handing over an envelope – 'and said to tell you to take note of its contents.'

Darius Gaynor waited until he was sitting near the whiskey ship before he opened the letter, which was written on official bakery stationery. In it Roberta Staunton insisted that he should not ask her to lunch again. From that day on she wished that their contact be limited strictly to business matters as it had been before. She had no objection to speaking to him on such terms, but she warned him that she would refuse any invitations to join him outside working hours. There was nothing in the letter which gave a specific reason why she had come to such a decision, but his antics on Friday could be the only explanation and in disgust at their impetuosity he punched himself quite hard on his lips. By the time he had returned to the office where Roberta Staunton worked, his lips were swollen slightly and the area around them was becoming red. The woman who had given him the letter asked if he had been attacked by drunken sailors, but he brushed aside the question and asked in vain if Roberta Staunton had returned. The messenger reminded him that she would not be back until three that afternoon – a response which drew nothing but muttered curses from Darius Gaynor.

In the yard outside he drove his truck as though reckless of life and exceeding the speed limit quite considerably. To those around who had come to know him as a gentle man with respect for the law, the sight of Darius Gaynor driving like a hooligan made no sense whatsoever. Some of them had to dive to safety as he tore through the gates and turned on to the road outside without any heed for the traffic already on it. It was lucky for him that there were no police about, otherwise his day would have taken still worse a turn, but even a confrontation with the law could scarcely have added to the rage with which he drove away.

At the earliest opportunity he had to consider dispassionately the letter which Roberta Staunton had written to him, Darius Gaynor tried to convince himself that she had written it in a hurry and without ample contemplation of the consequences of her actions. This was the only glimmer of hope he could find and, albeit a dim one, it allowed him to return to the Worthy Bakery some days later with at least the possibility that she would have had a change of heart. Whatever light emanated from that faint hope was quickly extinguished when she reiterated, to his face, the contents of her note. 'I've nothing to add to my letter,' she said. 'Nothing has changed since I wrote it.'

What surprised him was not only the force with which she stated her case but also the tone of her answers. When she spoke to him, she did not even look at his eyes, though she had been able to stare right into them during their innocent kisses, and all the time she spoke to him about the end of their courtship she evasively shuffled the papers on her desk. What was most disturbing was that he sensed that this was not just a ploy to occupy her eyes. 'Won't you even have the decency to look at me when you say "no"?' he asked. But no matter how much he asked her to stop what she was doing and look at him, she refused to do so and he had no alternative but to leave the office and drive away.

During their next few meetings, Darius Gaynor tried to effect a change in her behaviour by himself acting in a dismissive way. When he went to deliver his paperwork he spoke no more than the few words which were necessary to complete the transaction, and he looked at everything else there was to look at except Roberta Staunton. Although neither of them looked at the other, they each felt that the other was not looking either. And so they acted this juvenile ritual as if to be caught looking at each other would be to be shamed. Neither did they engage in any of the pleasantries which Roberta Staunton had said she would be willing to entertain. There were no more jokes about the details of the paperwork; not a word was said about the weather or any of the great political events taking place in the world – nothing at all passed between them which was not integrally a part of their business affairs. And so it continued for one month.

Unable to stand such a masquerade, Darius Gaynor sought other business which did not require him to pay any further visits to the Worthy Bakery. His reputation for honesty soon found him new work delivering okra to the large grocery stores who had noticed an inexplicable increase in demand for this erstwhile exotica. But, much as he tried to keep from thinking about Roberta Staunton, it proved impossible to protect himself against her memory at all times. Indeed changing business from sultanas and ginger to okra made no difference: the very sight of these vegetables came to represent the collapse of their love-affair and he could not look at them without seeing her eyes staring into his as they pecked each other's lips. Even years after the event, Darius Gaynor could never abide the sight of okra, for it reminded him of that month of shattered love.

But what increasingly upset him was that he had never been given a reason why Roberta Staunton had turned against him. As time went by he became more convinced that his thrusting kiss could not, in itself, have been the reason for his rejection. If it had upset her so much then surely she would have hit him at the time, or at least at the first opportunity. But nothing like that had happened, and the chasm left by his inability to explain the cause of his unhappiness began to swallow him. He became irritable and bad-tempered. The slightest inconvenience would have him ranting at whoever was responsible, and if the culprit was not nearby then he would rant at someone else. In the space of three weeks he received four cautions from the police for dangerous driving. At the time it did not occur to him, but all of these altercations with the law had come on the days when he was carrying the exotic vegetables. It was as if they gave off some vapour that affected him, an unknown allergen which made his blood seethe with anger and filled his mouth with ludicrous obscenities.

Not until some weeks after he had first come under the scrutiny of the law did he realise that his cargo had been the common denominator in all of these incidents. It was realising this fact more than anything else which made Darius Gaynor determine to sort out once and for all the reason why Roberta Staunton had written him that awful letter. He cancelled his contracts to deliver the newly popular vegetables with the excuse that he found the produce affected his health and his doctor had advised him to seek alternative cargoes. On the same day, he went to the company whose sultanas and ginger he had handled with such distinction for many years and asked – no, begged – to be allowed to carry them again. After some head-scratching his wish was granted, and on the following Tuesday morning he filled his truck with one of his old consignments to be delivered to the Worthy Bakery.

When he took his invoice to the office where Roberta Staunton worked, she was the first person that he saw. Not having seen him for some weeks, she had abandoned the practice of looking away whenever the door opened. But her blasé attitude cost her her composure when she found herself staring straight at the face of Darius Gaynor on that Tuesday morning. Nothing she tried to do could hide the fact that she wanted to cry on seeing him. She didn't cry, but that was thanks to training and not truth, and he knew by looking at her that all he had to do was ask her to join him again at lunch-time to walk to where the whiskey ships were moored.

During that walk, Roberta Staunton told him why she had written such a letter of seemingly irreversible rebuke. 'I must tell you something,' she said, 'but only on condition that you understand that if you ever utter a word of it to anyone, you'll disgrace me in the eyes of the world and no power in heaven or on earth could ever make me think of you again with anything but loathing.'

'My lips are sealed,' he said.

She began by talking of her mother, Loretta English. During her teenage years, Loretta English had tinkered with boys in the innocent way which so many girls do. She had kissed many of them and, although she never admitted it, there was little doubt that she had gone further than that, but Loretta English had never given up her most precious gift which she kept for the man who would marry her. She first thought she had met such a man when she was twenty-one. His name was Benedict Prendergast, and he was a magician with a hurling-stick capable of the most elegant play. But it was not his athletic ability which attracted Loretta English, for she had little interest in sport. Rather, what she found so desirable in him was the gentleness which came over him whenever he stepped from the field. Even though his hands were often badly cut, his knuckles visible beneath the torn skin, there was nothing in his everyday demeanour which gave the slightest hint that he could play against the most flagrant lawbreakers who would happily have smashed his hands and his teeth was it not for his anticipation of their malice. Despite placing himself in such danger on regular occasions, Benedict Prendergast looked like a chaperoned child who was unaware of the cruel realities of the real world. It was this ability to subjugate the perils of living which attracted Loretta English to him.

That she did not marry Benedict Prendergast was neither the fault of Loretta English nor for the want of trying. Insofar as it was possible for a young woman to coax a man to marry, she did so, but the more she did the more she found that what she believed to be his unflappable nature was in fact a definite disinclination to place himself in any position which required him to make any decisions of long-term consequence. When she finally accepted that Benedict Prendergast was not going to marry her, Loretta English said her goodbyes to him and left him to his field game. What she was not to know at that time was that Benedict Prendergast's unwillingness to make such a decision was but a passing phase and that within three years of their separation he would marry. But that was of no use to Loretta English. She cast herself free of him in the dubious confidence that someone else would pull her from the water, but this credo did not stop her crying herself to sleep in the first nights of her freedom as she thought of nothing else but her procrastinating hurler and the passion which had been entombed by his flighty heart.

The man whom she thought might be able to replace Benedict Prendergast was Dominic Stakelum, the cinema projectionist. There was something about the ease with which he loaded the film on to the machine which made Loretta English think that there might be something interesting to him if only she could find out what it was. Spending all those hours on his own looking at the same films over and over with only the backs of a hundred heads as an alternative view did nothing to make Dominic Stakelum an instantly interesting person to talk to. He had no hilarious anecdotes about getting tangled in the film or falling asleep before a reel change, for he was so meticulous about his profession that nothing of that sort had ever happened to him. Indeed, sometimes Loretta English thought him too careful for his own good. But despite his lack of daring charisma, she found in him a man who was courteous beyond anyone she had ever known, and who lavished gifts on her to the limit of his purse as she was the first woman to treat him with any hint of impending love.

Loretta English believed that she could draw out of him the true character which hid behind his diligent exterior. She had often heard her mother speak of hardening off the ornamental tobacco seedlings which she grew in the kitchen before planting them in her garden in the spring, and Loretta English believed that she could similarly gradually accustom Dominic Stakelum to the world she knew – never rushing him but always making progress. She introduced him to her friends, who were always expectant of interesting stories when they heard he was the projectionist at the Magic Picture House, but were always disappointed by the poverty of his conversation. But Loretta English's patient attention to his personality did begin to show results. He took the hints which she had dropped with decreasing subtlety and arrived for work one evening having drunk several glasses of vodka. He duly fell asleep in his chair, to be woken by irate cinema-goers banging at the door of the projectionist's room demanding to be shown the ending of the film they had paid good money to see. At the time Dominic Stakelum did not enjoy the incident and feared for his safety, but he insisted on telling the story at every opportunity in the following months, and he found it provided the ideal opening to many conversations.

That she had been able to convince Dominic Stakelum that he could become interesting to people was a great fillip to Loretta English, but she never managed to get him to make things happen without prompting. He was a dilemma for her. Born with copious manners, his instinct was always to appear polite rather than familiar, and no matter how much she tried to generate the momentum of roguishness in him, Dominic Stakelum never progressed beyond mischief by request.

For Loretta English the eventual realisation of his limited personality began to outweigh the pleasure she felt in his company. She began to think forward to the days when his not unattractive body would start to fall apart, or when her own interest in it would diminish. Whichever of these eventualities came first would signal the beginning of a difficult time for her, a time for which nature held out no remedy. What would she do with him when he was just an ageing man who could not make her laugh? What would happen then? It was such thoughts which overrode her love for him, and she was convinced that it was only her being dishonest with herself about the intensity of that love which allowed her to even entertain considerations of ever living with Dominic Stakelum. At the end of their affair, they kissed and said goodbye, but in the days which followed Loretta English found herself crying less than she had done in the wake of Benedict Prendergast – a sure sign, she thought, of the ascendancy of sense over romance in her heart.

As if she had a phantom ailment for which no cause could be found, Loretta English discovered that she could no longer conjure up any passion towards the men she met. She thought that her hormones might be at fault and wondered if this signalled an inability to have children which might present itself in years to come. This idea was to prove incorrect, but at that time Loretta English was dumbfounded by the absence of the real passion which she had felt only for her first lover, Benedict Prendergast. It was as if he had stolen the capacity for passion from her, like a cat stealing a sleeping child's breath, perhaps regarding it as another sporting memento to go with his many medals and trophies. Wherever it had gone, Loretta English missed it sorely and she found that its absence adversely affected the judgements she made about potential suitors who presented themselves. In the months following her admission of failure to cure Dominic Stakelum of his debilitating timidity, Loretta English became a woman of diminishing taste. Over a period of five months she met, kissed and fought with a variety of men she would not have shared a train with in the days of heady love with Benedict Prendergast, or even in the hopeful days of Dominic Stakelum's apparently emerging personality.

The men she was to be seen with in this period had in common only a complete absence of redeeming qualities, but none of them succeeded in taking from Loretta English the one thing which remained a constant in her determination, that piece of flotsam which still drifted on from the days when she was a discerning woman. There was Sylvester Moynihan, a corrupt bank official who helped himself to several pence every day from his coin tray. His chicanery did not amount to anything more than this and had no reason as romantic as wishing to shower a lover with gifts of adornment, for there was no more ulterior motive behind the subterfuge which Sylvester Moynihan spun than the appeasement of his minuscule ambition which would one day have him boasting that he had robbed a bank of a thousand pounds without adding that it had been done over seventeen years in small instalments, until the day he was caught with a face redder than his hand and given his marching orders. Another of her escorts was Hector Daly, the succotash addict, who filled his belly to the brim every day and spent the remainder of the time belching and farting. Nothing could live comfortably in the vicinity of Hector Daly, and within two weeks of their meeting Loretta English had moved to a different city in the name of her health, for she could not abide the thought of existing in the same jurisdiction as such an ignoramus.

These were the kinds of men in whose company Loretta English spent her time in the absence of the guiding hand of passion, a period brought to an end when she believed that she had felt that force again when she first saw Neddy Staunton walking in the rain with a mackintosh on and his bottom lip projected to form a cup to stop the water that ran down his face carrying on down his chin and the front of his neck. That was in November, when the rain always fell the heaviest and made the gutters overflow so it was impossible to cross the street without long leaps at either side of the road. Even in later years, Loretta English found it impossible to say why she had been struck by this man. He was not handsome, he was not handsome at all. That is not to say that he was ugly, but he had a plainness about his face which she would at one time in her life have sympathised with him for. He looked like a million other men, and it was perhaps a sign of the deterioration in the selectivity of Loretta English that she allowed her heart to surrender to such a person.

The mechanism by which she engineered their first meeting was unknown. Loretta English had never told her daughter about how it happened. In her earlier years Roberta Staunton had seen nothing amiss with this, as she did not think it right for a mother to divulge in any detail the manner in which she had paraded herself to her child's father. That was a secret of marriage which children had no business knowing. Looking back, Roberta Staunton wished she had been more insistent with her mother but it was too late now, as her mother was dead and her father was nowhere to be seen. There was nothing to be done about it now, and the young woman accepted her ignorance of the liaison's beginnings as she did the mousey-coloured hair and the double-jointed knuckles it had bequeathed to her. But always she carried with her, and more than ever as her age increased, a growing conviction that the early meetings between her mother Loretta English and her father Neddy Staunton had been in dismal circumstances, for the marriage which followed was never blessed with anything in the way of gentleness, and Roberta Staunton could best describe its legacy to her as 'Come from the dark, live in the dark.'

In the years up to Neddy Staunton's disappearance, years which numbered fifteen, Roberta Staunton had been the centre of her father's sexual attention. Whatever it was he needed to soothe his desires he did not find it in Loretta English, and instead of the child haphazardly wandering into her parents' bedroom it was the other way round – except there was nothing accidental about her father's visits. 'Come from the dark, live in the dark,' was how Roberta Staunton again described it to Darius Gaynor, who had occasionally heard that such things happened, but had never thought that he would meet someone who had been involved in such things, no more than he was likely to meet a film star. In the light of what he now knew, Darius Gaynor was ashamed of the impertinence he had shown on the day when he stole a larger kiss than he should have done. He was angry with himself for not foreseeing the possibility that such actions would be too frisky for someone who had been through what Roberta Staunton had been, but he eased his guilt with the sincerity of his intentions on that day and the fact that no one could be expected to detect signs of such victimisation and tread their way lightly in the remote possibility that the person they were in love with had been the subject of such illegal attention. Yet despite such vindication he remained angry with himself without quite knowing why.

In the days following that momentous journey to the whiskey ship, Darius Gaynor continued to take Roberta Staunton to walk by the quays. Despite her having divulged such an extraordinary story, they did not speak about it any more, at her insistence. 'All that is behind me now,' she said to him.

There was no immediate change in her personality in the aftermath of her tale, but Darius Gaynor did begin to notice, over a period of months, that Roberta Staunton was becoming more at ease when they were alone together. He noticed that when he kissed her on the cheeks she would turn her head more and more to the front so that with each passing month their lips came closer and closer. Like the astronomer Galileo he one day calculated that if the rate of turn continued as it was, they would again kiss properly by May. In fact it took longer than that, for closing the last gap took as long as all of the previous moves together and his calculations were out by two months. But the day did at last arrive when after walking together at lunch-time they returned to the spot where they said their good-byes and he found her head at the correct position to place a soft kiss on the front of her lips. And what was more, when he opened his eyes at the end of it, hers were firmly shut and he knew that at last he had succeeded in making her happy. He closed his own eyes again as she was clearly not finished, and they remained together for several minutes. It was nothing at all exhibitionist – just a long quiet meeting of lips and closing of eyes. Darius Gaynor had no idea at that time if this would be as far as they would get, but that did not bother him for she made him immensely happy and to see her rehabilitation progress in such a quantitative way gave him all the satisfaction he needed.

Chapter Four

Beneath the weight of her elegance which she wore about her like a carapace Grainne Dearvla Feherty was a decent woman. She bore in her head no ideas of malice which were measurably more sinister than was normal for a woman of her age and social position. What was unusual about Grainne Dearvla Feherty was that she could not prevent herself from acting above her station when in the company of others, lifting her head high into the air so she looked down at them and spoke through her harpoon nose. Holding her torso in such a position, it seemed only natural that she spoke in a tone consistent with her bearing and so she had become known as a snob. What was more the pity for Grainne Dearvla Feherty was that this portrayal of her, although physically understandable, was inaccurate as a reflection of the kind of woman she was.

She had been born tall. When she was delivered the nurse did not record her weight but her height, which was over two feet. A note was also taken of the immensely long and thin proboscis which the infant had, her head emerging from her mother's vagina looking like a watering-can. It was perhaps the young child's physique which gave those teaching her the idea that she should be brought up as a snob. She certainly had the physical attributes for such a role, so, as if by some cruel joke of peripatetics, the young child was taught to walk with her head back and her chin out. This was the cause of many accidents during her first few months of mobility, for she could not see where she was going and made a habit of crashing into things. She was also instructed to keep her mouth tightly shut when it was not in use and, during those times when it was closed, to purse her lips so that the orifice kept a circular shape which would in time be likened to a auck's arse. The young Grainne Dearvla Feherty was also brought up to speak in the first person as often as was credibly possible. Everyone got to know how she felt about things. It did not matter whether her opinions were of any relevance, and they certainly need not be of any interest to anyone else, but she would never let an opportunity pass without saying how she felt about this and that. This was a sad thing to happen to a child. What was puzzling about the case was that no one who had any influence over the way she was reared seemed to realise what was happening. It appeared that everyone was being led by the physique of the girl to give her a personality to match her longbow back and watering-can head.

When she was a young child the nature of her snobbishness was not so apparent to other children, who had still no concept of station. It was only when they reached the age of reason that quarrels broke out between Grainne Dearvla Feherty, and her fellow students. The attacks which began to be made on her were of a premeditated nature, as it became obvious to those who had to share classrooms with her that this was no ordinary girl with whom they could laugh as regularly as they argued; rather, this was a girl whom they could not bring themselves to like in any way. She did not

81

become a member of any faction for there were none who would allow themselves to be regarded as friends of Grainne Dearvla Feherty, and so as her isolation increased so too did her ability to shield herself from it by the construction of a massively elegant exterior of fashionable clothes which intimidated as much as it protected. Inside this fortress of couture, Grainne Dearvla Feherty existed in a rarefied atmosphere which would not have sustained anyone else. As she grew older, she began to amass a considerable collection of garments which reinforced the already widely held opinion that she was no ordinary woman. She never looked beautiful in her lavish clothes – her nose was far too big for that – but she was distinctive, and that in itself began to bring her a respectability which, though it never engendered affection, eventually exterminated the last remnants of the physical violence which she had once been all too prone to.

Despite the treatment which she had been subjected to in her formative years, Grainne Dearvla Feherty never looked upon the world as being ill-disposed towards her. Quite the opposite was the case, for though there was no reason why she should feel that way, Grainne Dearvla Feherty grew up believing that she was in some way indebted to the world. She spent many a day inside her clothes thinking about why this should be. Her nights too were occupied by constant deliberations on this, and these became an ever-present part of her psyche, but she could never find a reason. After some years, when she was in her mid fifties, she thought it was pointless to continue with this obsession and tried to put it to the back of her mind and to concentrate instead on the development of her elegance. But despite the success she had with this latter objective, there were always moments when her attention would be completely hijacked by the search for the reason for her guilt.

The tragedy of Grainne Dearvla Feherty was that she knew that even if she did come up with a theory for the way she felt, it would be of no real advantage to her in terms of melting the arctic feelings which her neighbours held towards her. For although she had a benevolent disposition, she was ill-equipped to exercise this as the very sight of her elegance frightened people away and she often thought that she might as well be a leper with a bell, clearing the streets as she went on her way.

Because of her affliction, Grainne Dearvla Feherty was confined to practising her generosity anonymously. Down through the years she had donated a very considerable amount of money to various causes. She had never taken the trouble to calculate exactly how much she had given, as she felt that to do so would be vulgar, but occasionally – just occasionally, when she was feeling devilish in herself – she would make a quick estimate based on her average weekly donations multiplied by her age, a calculation which always left her smiling. This satisfaction was usually enough to placate her, but there were times when she sought more concrete proof of her patronage. On those occasions she would take the train to the capital where, at least, her presence did not arouse such feelings of unease. There she would visit some of the institutions which had been the constant recipients of her anonymous bank drafts. Some of these places had walls too high to allow any view of the interior, so she would simply walk around outside listening for any sounds which might emanate. Sometimes she would hear something – a voice calling a name, a laugh, a shout, a dog barking – but this didn't matter to her, for she was happy enough just to see that these places were still functioning and she would privately congratulate herself on her secret munificence.

Visiting 'her' institutions, as she liked to think of them, was a great source of replenishment for Grainne Dearvla Feherty. On her return she would have the urge to confound her public image and smile at someone, but when she succumbed the grin would fall unheeded like a tree in the forest because the intended recipient would always have looked away. Grainne Dearvla Feherty had probably saluted almost everyone in the town at one time or another, but few of them were aware of it.

For a long part of her life she was satisfied enough with her lot. She contented herself with the knowledge that she had never done anything to harm a single thing, and she knew that her generosity far exceeded that of all of the participants in the annual displays of conspicuous charity which took place every Christmas. To those endeavours she contributed only enough to keep the reputation of miser from her door, but in truth she despised the indulgent motives behind them with an acerbity which was unusual for her.

But as she became an older woman and her body became less successful at resisting the influence of gravity, a feeling began to swell up inside Grainne Dearvla Feherty which could not be fed by her visits to the institutions in the capital city. She tried desperately to calm it with her journeys, walking around the walls of 'her' institutions like a pilgrim with her hands clasped against her sagging breasts and her mouth wording silent incantations which could have been mistaken for prayers but were nothing more than reminders of the way things used to be in the days of her comforting generosity. There were occasions when

Grainne Dearvla Feherty would spend hours in this state, circling and recircling the walls of some asylum in a desperate search for inner peace, but this was not to be found, and she would return home with her back bending over as it had rarely done since she had been born, the result of exhaustion and disappointment at yet another wasted day.

What Grainne Dearvla Feherty could not subdue was the feeling that she was a grossly misunderstood woman and that the passage of time was robbing her of opportunities to make it known that she was not an elegant snob and that the length of her nose and the shape of her back no more made her a callous woman than the outstretched hands made the Christmas beggars irredeemable from poverty. What worried her most was that the creeping anxiety which had begun to possess her might fulfil the prophecies which had always been made about her and she would indeed become the venomous cobra that many had believed her to be from birth. That would be the most terrible thing, she thought to herself, but she had no idea how to save herself and there was no one to turn to for advice.

For the first time in her life Grainne Dearvla Feherty felt truly alone. No longer had she the realisation of her discreet generosity to comfort her. This had been the only true companion she had had, but now it too was abandoning her. She fell behind in her contributions, the effort of going to her bank proving too troublesome for her. Her appearance became unkempt when she was indoors. When she went out she still prepared herself beforehand, as she struggled to prevent her internal turmoil becoming public knowledge, but it was all becoming so much of an effort. She even tried to drink alcohol, from a bottle of whiskey which had stood for twenty years at the back of her ornamental glass cabinet. It was her first encounter with the liquid, and the taste was so foul that she emptied the bottle down the sink as soon as she had wiped the vomit from her mouth. It seemed that there was nothing she could do to avert the advancing depression which threatened to engulf her, and her outward appearance of elegance was no longer to protect her from the ignorance of others but only to contain the disintegration of her mind, just as a dam contains water.

In the few remaining weeks of sanity which she believed were left to her, Grainne Dearvla Feherty knew that there was nothing she could do on her own to end the torments which were suffocating her. She had said all that there was to say to herself. In the previous months the cupboard of consolation had been emptied, and she felt that within a few weeks her mind would be irrevocably submerged in distress. Any assistance she would then receive would simply be to arrange for her entry into one of the institutions she had so generously supported for a very long time. But her reasons for doing so had never been to prepare those places for her arrival, of that she was unquestionably certain, and she could only slightly arrest her advancing catastrophe by the anger she felt at the very idea that someone might deliver her to the gates of one of those awful places and feel that they were performing an act of great charity. It might even happen at Christmas. Such a spectre filled Grainne Dearvla Feherty with such contempt that she tried to purge it by hurling herself against the walls of the living-room which had been the location for some of the most contented reflections on her munificence in the past. What was equally frightening for her was the knowledge that she would have to go to someone outside to ask for help. Nothing in her past life had given her the slightest inkling of how that should be done. She was not sure if to seek help would constitute failure, but she knew that the alternative would certainly not lead to success. Neither did she know if to seek help would constitute a betrayal, but it seemed that such an act entailed so great a break with what she was used to that it must, somehow or another, require her abandoning some principle, because it certainly meant an abandonment of a whole way of life. Grainne Dearvla Feherty had not the slightest idea of what principle she would be rejecting in her search for an outside mentor, but, whatever it was, the consequences of not doing it would, she knew, be nothing short of an undeserved tragedy for her.

The morning she had allotted as the time to go and talk to someone was warm and dry. Grainne Dearvla Feherty rose at eight o'clock as was normal for her. She had not slept well the night before as was also usual on the eve of a major event. During the early hours her thoughts were constantly drifting back to when she was a schoolgirl and the unease which always accompanied the night before an important examination. That was exactly how she felt that night, and in many ways it served to heighten the distress she felt at how much time had been wasted in the years since her childhood. Grainne Dearvla Feherty did not entirely blame herself for that waste, for it was obvious that others were as guilty as she for the circumstances in which she now found herself. At breakfast there was toast and a poached egg washed down with tea. Her meals had always been spartan as she had a very low threshold for gluttony. When she had eaten and washed the dishes, Grainne Dearvla Feherty climbed the stairs to her room and began the two-hour ritual of constructing her elegance. The bottles of ointments made her dressing-table look like an alchemist's laboratory. In her wardrobe hung thirty-six dresses from which she would select her attire for that day. The anointing and the selection was done with the sobriety of a buyer at a horse fair: each and every alternative was studied with caution; nothing was left to chance.

Shortly after eleven o'clock Grainne Dearvla Feherty was satisfied that it was not possible to improve further on her appearance. Before leaving the room she took one last long look at herself in the full-length mirror she had had installed in the early days of her elegance, and watching herself in it she had no idea if it would be the last time she would appear before it in such splendour. After that she went downstairs. In her usual way she then made a tour of the house to see that everything was where it should be, for there was still nothing disturbed her more than to return home and find that something had been out of place for her entire absence. When that was done, Grainne Dearvla Feherty searched beneath the stairs for the tiny bottle in the shape of the Virgin Mary which had been put there ten years before on the death of her mother. She had some difficulty opening it, but once this was done she quickly upturned the bottle so that a sprinkling of holy water gathered at Lourdes wetted the tip of her index finger. With it she made the sign of the cross on her forehead for the first time in a decade. Then she re-placed the bottle beneath the stairs, took one last look around her and walked out the front door.

Gretchen Gaynor was again in her front garden, where the sight of her backside had become as integral a part of the view as the flowers and bushes themselves. Her back was no longer as supple as it used to be, so when anyone went by and called out a greeting to her she did not straighten up to return the sentiment but instead muttered a reply from her working position. She was such a popular figure that to stand up every time she was saluted would have left her with no time to work. In any case she knew everyone by the sound of their voices and so did not have to look to put a name to the salutes. That morning she had been staking her sweet peas for almost an hour and was feeling quite bored with it. She was bent over with her backside facing the road when a voice called to her which she did not recognise. Sometimes this did happen if the caller spoke too low or their words coincided with a noise in the distance. In such cases Gretchen Gaynor would simply say 'Good day to you,' and leave it at that. That is exactly what she said this time. 'Good day to you,' she said, expecting that to be the end of it. But it was not. The voice called her name again. 'Gretchen, have you got a minute of your time?' it said. So Gretchen had no alternative but to begin the painful straightening of her back which she was sure was becoming riddled with rheumatism. When she stood up and turned around she could not believe her eyes. It was no wonder she had not recognised the voice, for there stood the tall and elegant figure of Grainne Dearvla Feherty, a woman she had not spoken to for thirty years. She was dressed in a long grey outfit which reached down to the tops of her narrow ankles. Around her shoulders she had laid a burgundy shawl, matched by the embroidered gloves on her hands and a fantastic cavalier's hat whose lace mantilla shielded her trembling lips. From a distance she was a movie star, but as Gretchen Gaynor walked nearer to her she was able to tell with the certainty of an iridologist from the condition of the lady's eyes that Grainne Dearvla Feherty was a woman in distress.

'Do you think I could see your husband?' said Grainne Dearvla Feherty, her petrified voice exposing the grief within. 'Could I see him now, please?'

Gretchen Gaynor did not know what to think, for although she had not been among the elegant woman's most vociferous critics, she had shared the general belief that Grainne Dearvla Feherty was a snob. 'There is someone with him at the moment,' she replied. 'Perhaps if you came back later . . . maybe in an hour.'

Grainne Dearvla Feherty's immediate instinct was to accept this suggestion with relief, but she quickly remembered the difficulty she had had in coaxing herself to come this far and did not think that she could do so again. In the midst of this thought she remembered her visions of being delivered to the gates of an asylum at Christmas by a hypocrite and so she could not accept Gretchen Gaynor's offer. 'No, no,' she said in a growing panic. 'That's out of the question – impossible. I have to see him now . . . soon. Perhaps I could wait in your house. I think that would be fine, if you don't mind.'

Gretchen Gaynor could see nothing wrong with such an idea except the unease she would feel at having this woman beneath her roof, but she consented and escorted Grainne Dearvla Feherty towards the kitchen. Then she changed her mind, as she felt the kitchen was too humble a place for the elegant woman to sit, so instead she led her to the living-room and invited her to sit down, enquiring if she would like some tea.

Grainne Dearvla Feherty sat by the window for some time. Gretchen Gaynor had brought her some tea and had then made the excuse of having to return to her plants to complete their staking as rain was predicted for the afternoon. The truth behind her departure however was that she knew that to sit with the elegant woman would be to remain in an awkward silence, for there was not a single thing that they would have to say to each other. From where she sat, Grainne Dearvla Feherty could hear the murmur of voices from upstairs. She tried to gauge the level at which to speak so that only Linus Gaynor would be able to hear what she had to say and not anyone who might come to the door to earwig. All kinds of scenarios began to ferment in her mind. The most insistent one was that Gretchen Gaynor had left her alone not to return to her plants but to run about the town whispering that a most startling thing had happened and that Grainne Dearvla Feherty, the most elusive woman any of them had ever known, was at that very moment sitting by the window in her living-room with an appointment to see Linus Gaynor. The elegant woman could only begin to imagine the reaction that such a revelation would bring, and it hurt her considerably to think of the speculation that would erupt as to the reason for her extraordinary visit. This was indeed a graphic sign of the collapse of the high masquerade which had surrounded her since childhood, and she felt naked without its protection. She had never before felt so vulnerable, and she was only glad that Gretchen Gaynor had left her alone, for she could not prevent herself from crying and stooping her head as she did so – the breakdown of her resolve being reflected in the buckling of her physique. In fact, however, Gretchen Gaynor had been true to her word, and as the elegant woman sat crying by the window the wife of Linus Gaynor was paying attention to nothing but the staking of her sweet peas in advance of the rain.

91

Grainne Dearvla Feherty had been waiting for most of an hour when she heard the sound of footsteps upstairs, followed by the opening of a door and the voices of two men on the stairs. She sat completely silent so as not to alert anyone to her presence. The voices were those of Ignatius Phelan and Setanta Bermingham, brother of Milo the fiddler, who had come for some adjudication in a dispute regarding standing fees owed following the birth of a crippled foal. Neither of them detected the presence of the elegant woman in the living-room as they passed the door into the front garden to bid Gretchen Gaynor goodbye.

Grainne Dearvla Feherty was not sure of what to do now, and for some moments she waited in the hope that Gretchen would come and get her. For a few minutes there was no sign of anyone coming, and Grainne Dearvla Feherty was about to stand up and leave the room when she heard the front door close and the approaching footsteps of Gretchen Gaynor. The two stood looking at each other for a moment, then Gretchen explained what was to be done: that the problem was first to be described in as much detail as was possible and then Linus was to be left alone to reach his decision. Grainne Dearvla Feherty nodded her head in acceptance of the procedure without explaining that she had not come for any kind of ruling.

The two women mounted the stairs and stood outside the door at the top. Then Gretchen Gaynor knocked lightly and entered, leaving the elegant woman outside. After a few moments she returned to the landing and ushered the visitor into the bedroom, closing the door behind her.

When she heard the click of the latch which told her that the door was properly shut, Gretchen Gaynor walked down the stairs and back into her garden. She would have dearly loved to know what it was which brought Grainne Dearvla Feherty to see her husband, and perhaps in another time she would have flattened her ear against the door to listen to what was being said behind it. But she was a disciplined acolyte by now, and years of escorting people to see her husband had instilled in her a religious respect for privacy which could not be overruled by inquisitiveness. So although Grainne Dearvla Feherty's arrival gave her more cause for wonderment than was usual, she stuck to her honourable routine and contented herself with speculation.

It was while she was speculating that Meabh Slevin came to her. She had seen Grainne Dearvla Feherty enter the house from the excellent observation position in her bedroom window and could not resist the temptation to come running down the street to ask what the elegant woman wanted. 'Surely you know something,' she said to Gretchen. 'She must have said something to you – anything at all.'

In all, Grainne Dearvla Feherty spent two hours with Linus Gaynor. Gretchen was unable to gather any indication of what the trouble might be. In most cases which came before her husband, she was able to make some guesses based on the intonation of the voices. But this time she heard nothing, not even a low drone, and it could have been the case that the elegant woman sat by her husband's bed without saying a word to him. Gretchen Gaynor even went back into her house on spurious journeys just to see if she could hear anything, but she could not and so she returned to her plants and her speculation. When Grainne Dearvla Feherty did eventually come down, she had little to say for herself. Passing Gretchen in the garden, she thanked her for the hospitality and asked if it would be convenient for her to return in a few days. When she was assured that this would be fine, the elegant woman said a quick goodbye and crossed the road on her way home.

The news that Grainne Dearvla Feherty had been to see Linus Gaynor did not take long to be known by everyone who lived within miles of his house. On her mission of gossip, Meabh Slevin had taken to her bicycle to spread the word, believing that even her legs, long used to running everywhere, would be inadequate to the task of spreading such important news to all who must hear it. She rode past the field where Derek and Seorse Bermingham, brothers of Milo, were pilfering spinach and shouted at them that the elegant bitch had been to see Linus Gaynor. She woke up the mechanic Eamonn McDermott McDermott who had fallen asleep beneath Monty Contello's car to tell him the news. 'You won't believe this,' she said, 'but Grainne Dearvla Feherty has been to see Linus Gaynor. God have mercy on us all but something terrible is going to happen. I can feel it in me waters.' She even called on Iggy Quinn to tell him. He, it must be said, was flattered even to receive a visit from Meabh Slevin, as he was not used to people going out of their way to speak to him (which was entirely due to his dreadful breath, which smelt of mustard). Having circulated the news within an hour, Meabh Slevin returned again to the house of Linus Gaynor to enquire if Gretchen had been able to glean further information. But she had not, and so everyone had to content themselves with communal conjecture, at which they had such experience.

Despite the absence of information, an abundance of theories was put forward as to why Grainne Dearvla Feherty had gone to see Linus Gaynor. All of these ideas were expanded and intermeshed and perhaps through luck, as it was unlikely to be through rational argument, from this long process the truth emerged that she had gone to see him because she could no longer bear the isolation in which she had lived for so long. During the few days it took for this consensus to evolve, the elegant woman was not seen once. Since she had closed the door of her house on returning from seeing Linus Gaynor, she had not set foot outside it again. But even from within her walls she could feel the attention of eyes on her, and in later years she would recount how the plaster in the rooms was lukewarm to the touch in those days of extreme exile.

Grainne Dearvla Feherty waited indoors as if in obedience to some law of nature while the form of her salvation took shape in the head of Linus Gaynor. She felt herself detained there by instinct, as if to emerge prematurely would violate a process which had taken such courage to begin. She lived on meagre rations, having little food stored to begin with, and despite her feeble appetite she did not have enough to eat. But Grainne Dearvla Feherty did not complain. Instead she immersed herself in thought and inactivity, sleeping very little as if to expel some terrible beast from her body by making it an impossible place in which to dwell. When she did re-emerge, her face was gaunt and pale. Her long nose seemed to droop more than usual, and the bones in her hands were visible through the skin like an X-ray. But what was most startling about Grainne Dearvla Feherty's appearance was that she was not elegant. This may have been due to amnesia brought on by exhaustion, or perhaps she was consciously rejecting the necessity for elegance in her life any more, but this was a woman unrecognisable from the one which had walked into the house some days earlier. She was indeed a frightening sight, and some of the children who saw her complained of nightmares for weeks afterwards.

When she reached the house of Linus Gaynor, Grainne Dearvla Feherty had to be helped up the stairs by Gretchen Gaynor, who was upset by the sight of this gaunt woman. Then, just as she had done a few days before, Gretchen Gaynor did no more than show Grainne Dearvla Feherty into her husband's bedroom and close the door behind her before going back to her garden. There, numerous faces were turned towards her from over the front fence and from the doors and windows in the houses nearby, all of them expecting her to say something about the erstwhile glamorous woman, but she had nothing to report. From where they stood in the garden and in the street outside, nothing could be heard from the room. Just as before, there was not even a low drone and others came to the same opinion that Grainne Dearvla Feherty must indeed be sitting in silence beside Linus Gaynor, just taking succour from his presence.

Grainne Dearvla Feherty stayed with Linus Gaynor for an unusually long period of time. A second visit was normally much briefer than the first as it only required a few questions to be posed and the blinking of his eyes to answer them. But Grainne Dearvla Feherty had stayed for well over an hour before those outside heard the sound of the door opening, at which point they ran for cover – some of them behind the shrubs, others behind cars and others again behind the doors of their houses from where they peered round the jambs to see the once elegant woman emerge into the garden. But it was only those who crouched behind the near bushes who heard what she had to say. 'I believe there has been a miracle,' she said to Gretchen. 'I am filled with the Holy Spirit.' They looked at each other for confirmation of what they had heard, but there was no doubt that Grainne Dearvla Feherty had come into the garden looking replenished and smiling and saying to Gretchen that she believed there had been a miracle.

The miracle that Grainne Dearvla Feherty spoke of was nothing to do with a physical healing, for she had no need of such a cure. What she spoke of was the courage she had gained from spending time in the presence of Linus Gaynor. She confirmed what many had surmised: namely, that not a word had been spoken to him. That, however, had not been by intention, for, despite her almost complete isolation from those who lived near her, she had been able to deduce the manner in which Linus Gaynor administered justice from the fragments of conversations she overheard, and during the days before her first visit to him Grainne Dearvla Feherty had rehearsed time and again the things she would say. She had written them on a piece of paper so that the nervousness she knew would affect her would not strike her dumb with aphasia. But that was not how it had worked out. No sooner had Gretchen Gaynor closed the door behind her, leaving her alone in the presence of Linus Gaynor, than she felt it unnecessary to say a word. She kept the piece of paper with the chronology of her life in her hand without opening it once during the entire visit. She sat on the chair by his head and knew that he understood why she had come. It was a time the like of which Grainne Dearvla Feherty had never had before. In all of two hours not a word was said, but the more she stayed there the more she felt he came to understand her plight. 'It was a meeting of minds in the purest sense of the phrase,' she said. 'I never said a word, and yet it felt like a long monologue of the most intimate kind. Simply sitting beside him and thinking to myself of the state of my life seemed to help transfer the burden, and I was never in any doubt but that he knew what I would have said if I had opened my mouth.'

On her second visit to see Linus Gaynor, Grainne Dearvla Feherty had remained in equal silence. 'I knew what he was thinking because I had come to the same conclusion myself, namely that I had to end my isolation from the world and begin to speak to people again. I sat for an hour beside him without looking into his eyes, and when I felt that I was ready I stood up and bent over and stared down at him. What I was looking for was confirmation that I was right, and he blinked once at me. At that moment I felt a real warmth return to my body. I had not felt such a thing since I was a child. It was wonderful, not because I knew what had to be done but because I felt I had the ability to do it.'

It was certainly true that Grainne Dearvla Feherty was a changed woman who could now speak with ease to anyone she wished to. What was more, no one found her conversations exhibitionist in the wake of her cure. No indeed – she could now speak and make others completely at ease with her company. Another of the consequences of her transformation was the sale of her thirty-six elegant dresses, the money from which she used to pay a craftsman to redecorate her house in a burst of extravagant colours.

From the day of her second visit onwards, Grainne Dearvla Feherty walked about as living proof of the miraculous powers of Linus Gaynor. Her case was to be a watershed, for it marked the beginning of a gradual change in the things which people came to see him about. Whereas before the metamorphosis in the character of Grainne Dearvla Feherty, Linus Gaynor had been seen as the seat of efficient justice, he increasingly became the focus for those seeking cures to more intractable problems.

The evidence of the powers of Linus Gaynor was most graphically displayed by the public speeches which now became a part of Grainne Dearvla Feherty's day. The woman who at one time could barely bring herself to speak to her reflection in a mirror was now spending her evenings standing in church halls reliving the moment of her cure by Linus Gaynor. She spoke with such aplomb that she converted even those who came to her dissertations with a mountain of scepticism. As they had never met her before, how were they to know that this woman was not a consummate liar? But in addition to the eloquence of her speeches they also contained the watermark of unmistakable truth. She travelled like a disciple for hundreds of miles from her home, drawing large crowds who stood in lengthy ovation when she had finished. During these appearances her advice was sought by many who thought that Linus Gaynor might be able to fill them with the same feeling of self-respect which he had endowed on Grainne Dearvla Feherty. Bad musicians came to her wondering if he would be able to guide their fingers. Dancers came seeking help for their feet, accountants who had problems with addition, lazy housewives who were allergic to dust and many others who felt that their lives had become insignificant and needed a change.

In all, Grainne Dearvla Feherty spent a year on this tour, which she looked upon as a mission of vocation. Though she could not be certain, she estimated that she spoke to a hundred thousand people in that time, most of whom came merely to see a woman who had become something of a circus attraction, but a small minority of whom were deeply in need of help.

Having heard her speak, many of what might be called these mental cripples arrived at the house of Linus Gaynor, but their numbers were too large for them to be allowed in, and so an area was set aside beneath his window where they could stand and kneel in the hope that his healing powers would trickle over the tops of the hollyhocks and down on top of them. The gravel surface which had been specially laid so these unfortunates would not have to stand in the muck did not last long. It disappeared in small stages, taken as relics to be rubbed on the foreheads or placed under the pillows of the bewildered. Its demise caused some anger, as it had been an expensive amenity, and so it was replaced by a concrete square measuring ten feet by twenty.

There were small-time entrepreneurs who saw in the pilgrims an opportunity to make some money. The most common venture was to sell hot water to them for a farthing a kettle. In the summertime, when the number of visitors was at its highest, the street where Poule stood became a strip of hot-water merchants, price-cutting each other out of business until Fergus Bermingham, the largest brother of Milo, imposed a cartel and threatened to break the head of anyone who started another price war.

Enormous Father Raymond Curtis did not know what to make of this new phenomenon. He had no difficulty with Linus Gaynor's having replaced incompetent judges as the sole arbiter on matters of law, but his growing reputation as a worker of miracles did not sit comfortably with the huge man of the cloth. At first he was tempted to ignore those who came and pilfered the gravel path beneath Linus Gaynor's window. To look at them they presented no cause for concern, for they comprised such bewildered specimens that they would, he thought, not recognise a miracle if it happened to them. He presumed that in time the inaccessibility of the town and the lack of further cures would reduce the numbers to a small group of hopefuls, and that eventually no one would come any more.

But despite the hopes of Father Raymond Curtis, which he supplemented with frequent praying in his confessional, the number of pilgrims who came to stand on the concrete path outside Linus Gaynor's bedroom did not decline. The only response to the priest's prayers seemed to be the lack of any further accounts of miraculous cures. This relieved Father Raymond Curtis more than it surprised him, for he knew that Grainne Dearvla Feherty had not been the recipient of divine intervention but had merely realised that she had to do something to prevent her decline . into oblivion. Faced with such a choice, the priest felt that she had done nothing more than any normal human being would have done. What increasingly concerned him was the possibility that some of those who came to stand outside Linus Gaynor's bedroom would undergo a recovery which in truth was due to nothing more than hysteria. The possibility of such a claim was increased by the fact that all of those who came were seeking solutions to mental problems. Had they been polio victims or dying from tuberculosis, as many thousands were doing at the time, then any reported cure could be substantiated. But the absence of verifiable physical symptoms made things very tricky as far as Father Raymond Curtis was concerned. He regarded many of those who came as no more than layabouts and vagabonds. That one of these might be stricken by a sudden surge of conscience brought on by the intensity of the place was a distinct possibility. That was all it would take to bring thousands more to Poule, beating their breasts and chanting hymns in thanks for a non-existent cure.

Father Raymond Curtis began to believe that the possibility of such an event was dangerously high, but all he could do was refuse to give the visits the support of his presence. From the day the pilgrims first began to arrive he became a less frequent visitor to Poule, and when he did go there to administer the Blessed Sacrament to Linus Gaynor, which never went beyond wetting his lips with altar wine, it was always at night. On these visits the priest kept his suspicions to himself, responding with faked surprise to comments about his recent scarcity. He would arrive wearing a large coat with the collar pulled up high so it covered the sides of his face, and he sometimes thought that he must have looked like a customer entering a brothel. When he left Poule he would never return home straight away, for he would have arranged an appointment in the opposite direction so as to kill any direct trail between the presbytery and the house of Linus Gaynor, the supposed miracle-worker. Behaving in such a way did not make him feel good about himself. It angered him that he should have to act like a criminal, covering his steps to disguise his whereabouts, but he preferred it to the certainty of the trouble which would begin if one of the visitors (and that was as civilised as he was prepared to be about them) reported a similar transformation to Grainne Dearvla Feherty's, a woman for whom he no longer had any patience.

But despite the best prayers which Father Raymond Curtis had to offer, and all the words of invective he silently mouthed at the arriving pilgrims, his most earnest wish was not fulfilled. The catastrophe happened at a time when he thought that all was returning to normal. It had been almost a year since Grainne

Dearvla Feherty had proclaimed a miracle standing in the front garden of Linus Gaynor's house, and during that time her preaching had sent thousands to Poule to stand beneath the window. But despite the numbers that came, there had not been a single case which replicated her claim that Linus Gaynor was capable of interceding on behalf of those who believed in him. The passage of time had led Father Raymond Curtis to relax his fears. 'Surely,' he thought to himself, 'surely something would have happened by now.' He grew more confident that there would soon be an end to the nonsense about miracles through his gradual rationalisation that one of the mad pilgrims would have announced themselves cured at the earliest moment with no greater motive than to attract attention to themselves. But it had not happened. Nothing had happened and so the priest thought that after one year of this the whole masquerade would collapse through the inability of anyone to emulate the transformation of Grainne Dearvla Feherty. But it was not to be so. It was not to be so at all.

The event that enormous Father Raymond Curtis had always feared fell upon a Tuesday. It was a Tuesday in early November in fact, on a calm sunny day between a torrential Monday and a misty Wednesday. It was a beautiful afternoon with the sky half blue and half white cloud, and the priest was returning home after taking cabbages to the nuns who ran the home for the dying. Immediately he entered the outskirts of the town he could sense that something had happened. At a later stage he described how his stomach felt suddenly upset despite the unexceptional lunch he had eaten. In the town he was first approached by Meabh Slevin, who ran to his bicycle as quickly as she could and blocked him from going any further. She was beside herself with excitement but eventually managed to pass on the message that there had been a confirmed cure of a woman suffering from agoraphobia, who had now taken to sitting in the fields speaking to sheep. This very woman had stood on the concrete path beneath Linus Gaynor's window only a week before. Everyone swore they remembered her, though the accounts of her appearance differed widely. The news was greeted with such delight that the vendors gave away free hot water for ten minutes – having first checked to see how many people were about. Once again, Father Raymond Curtis had to conceal his true feelings. He joined in the words of wonder which filled the air at the time. People were congratulating each other, though why they deserved congratulation he did not know. But he shook hands anyway until he could make his exit without arousing any suspicions about his real concern for what would happen now.

In the privacy of his room, Father Raymond Curtis sat in the chair by the window and knew that his days of peace were over. In the previous year he had often thought of what he might do if he found himself faced with this situation. For all the time he had spent contemplating his actions in such an eventuality, sitting there in the middle of the real thing he knew that there was nothing that could prepare a man of his profession for an occasion like this. He knew the demands that would be made of him. Now that everyone seemed convinced that Linus Gaynor possessed some special gift of a spiritual origin, he would be expected to preside at numerous ceremonies which gave official credence to such a consensus. Like a good shepherd, he would be expected to lead the people in the celebration of this momentous man and to make whatever approaches were necessary to the powers that be to see

to it that the cause of Linus Gaynor received the bur-
eaucratic attention it deserved. That their enormous
priest did not believe the story had never occurred to
any of its promulgators. It had struck Father Raymond
Curtis as unusual that of the thousand people who had
come to stand on the footpath below Linus Gaynor's
window, not one – not even those he regarded as the
most discerning of the population – had ever asked him
if he believed the whole saga.

Being perfectly honest with himself, Father Raymond Curtis knew that his own inactivity in the early
days of the renewal of Grainne Dearvla Feherty had
been a mistake. If there had ever been a chance for him
to quell the hysteria it was then, before she took her
mouth all over the country to preach up this story of
intercession. He knew he should have spoken up
immediately. If he had done so, then perhaps – just
perhaps – he would have been able to renounce the
exegesis of the tale and kill it when it first saw the light
of day. His chance gone, he took out his special note-
paper and the pen given to him by a consortium of his
elderly relatives on his ordination and began to write to
his Bishop, who he knew would be incensed at what he
had to report. For there was nothing the Bishop hated
more than rumours of miraculous cures.

The Bishop's fear of such cases was that they meant
spending time and money on investigations. These
invariably resulted in a schism between those who
believed and those who did not. The Bishop had had
experience of this before, and it was his profound
conviction that such stories never had any foundation
and that their only contribution was trouble. In the
fearsome speeches he had often made to his clergy, he
had warned them again and again that they were never
to allow these kinds of thing to grow. Such rumours

were to be crushed immediately, and anyone found responsible for neglecting his duty in this respect would receive no mercy from him.

Father Raymond Curtis posted his account in the green letterbox from where he could see the light in the bedroom of Linus Gaynor, and he thought he heard a crash as the letter hit the bottom.

Chapter Five

Judge Olin Prescott could well believe his ears that morning, though he would very much have preferred not to. He had again been woken by the sound of his neighbour's youngest son practising his trumpet before breakfast, playing, as he had been doing for over six months, the chorus of 'Ba Ba Blacksheep' without any discernible improvement. The Judge got out of bed without speaking to or kissing his wife, for they had dispensed with such nonsense years before. Now if they spoke to each other first thing in the morning their conversations were about food or whether the weather required the Judge to wear his galoshes: there were never any greetings or enquiries after each other's health. The Judge then made his way downstairs and into the bathroom, where he spent the next twenty minutes making himself look beautiful.

This was becoming more and more difficult. For a start, his teeth had become a symphony of browns and greys, and no amount of scrubbing would make them look anything like they had been in his teens, but he continued to brush them in the conviction that they would at least be clean dirty. His hair too was no longer doing him any favours. There was not much of it any more, but he still contrived to have it cover most of his skull, meticulously separating the hairs and assigning them to different parts of his head like a mother dividing meagre rations among her children. This was after he had applied more hair dye with an old toothbrush – a treatment which made his hair colour completely incompatible with the tone of his skin and drew attention to it immediately anyone saw him, as if he wore a cat on his head.

When he was satisfied that he had done all that was possible with the resources available to him, Judge Olin Prescott ate his breakfast of lamb's liver and toast washed down with a mug of tea. Then he left the house, telling his wife, 'I will be home when I am home.'

The Judge had a long journey that morning, taking him over two hours to complete. But what was worse was the appalling state of the roads, which sent his car jolting about and so upsetting his hair that he had to stop occasionally to reset it properly. Driving past the house of Linus Gaynor, the Judge noticed a larger crowd than normal standing on the concrete path beneath the window. He paid no attention to this, dismissing them as misguided fools and refusing to give them the tribute of more than a glancing look. He parked his car outside the American Hotel as usual and crossed the road to the police station where he found Sergeant Donald Kilgallon practising his signature in an effort to make it consistently illegible. 'Very good, Sir,' said Judge Olin Prescott. 'You should be a bureaucrat with a scrawl like that.'

The Judge's unannounced entry had again caused the Police Sergeant embarrassment, and he quickly sat forward at his desk so that his forearms covered the paper on which he had been doodling. 'Good morning,

Your Honour,' he said, trying to stand up while still keeping his forearms flat on the desk, 'Conas tá tú?'

'I'm very well,' replied the Judge, 'but please don't try to ingratiate yourself with that native-tongue nonsense. We're all grown-ups here.'

Embarrassed by his aimless scribbling and sycophancy, the Police Sergeant attempted to slide the piece of paper into his wastebasket like a bad magician. He then tried to re-establish his credibility by offering the Judge some tea, but this move also failed, being met with a polite refusal and a request to be escorted to the Farmers' Hall so that the day's proceedings could begin.

Crossing the street with the Judge, the Police Sergeant tried to impress on him that he should not get his hopes up too high. In truth Donald Kilgallon knew that there would again be no cases for the Judge to hear and he tried to extend an advance apology in case the blame should fall on him. 'Things have been very quiet here since your last visit,' he grovelled. 'In fact I don't think I have heard of any major difficulty recently.'

Judge Olin Prescott remained uninterested in what the Sergeant had to say, concentrating instead on the sight of Meabh Slevin running quickly up the side of the street with her eyes at right angles to her nose as she looked across at the Judge and his escort.

Inside the Farmers' Hall, the Judge found his desk and chair exactly as he had left them some weeks before. 'There haven't been any concerts,' explained Donald Kilgallon wiping a fortnight's dust from the seat with his sleeve. Again he enquired if the Judge would take some tea, like offering a propitiatory tribute to an angry god, but the Judge refused and so the Sergeant left him alone and returned to his station, ordering himself not to do any more scribbling until the Judge was safely out of the town.

Police Sergeant Donald Kilgallon's low expectation of any cases for the Judge came as no surprise to Olin Prescott. As on his previous visit, he himself did not expect an early breakthrough in his efforts to regain jurisdiction for the authentic law. What he was seeking to do was to make it clear that he would not be deterred in his mission to establish once again the normality of official justice, no matter how bad a record it had and how much an improvement was the system which had replaced it. For Judge Olin Prescott the issue was one not of quality but of legality, and he was in no doubt as he sat alone in the big dusty Farmers' Hall that legality was on his side and the merits of its impartiality would in time subvert the rule of Linus Gaynor.

When she had run past the Judge and the Police Sergeant, looking at them with that painful twist of her eyeballs, Meabh Slevin ran to the house of Linus Gaynor. Gretchen was not in her garden, for she had finished her work for the winter. She was in fact in her scullery pickling onions when Meabh Slevin entered and then knocked on the door. 'The Judge is back,' she said. 'I've seen him with my own eyes crossing the road to the Farmers' Hall.'

Gretchen Gaynor did not react in the panicked fashion Meabh Slevin had hoped for. 'Well, we always knew he was coming back,' she replied.

Unable to arouse any consternation there, Meabh Slevin ran back out the door and up the street in search of someone who would share her hysteria, a task which fell to Gregory Bermingham, unfortunate brother of Milo the musician.

*

Judge Olin Prescott continued to sit at the desk on the stage of the Farmers' Hall in defiance of the outrageous improbability that anyone would come to seek his opinion on a matter of law. He had again brought plenty of paperwork with him to occupy his time, though he diverted himself more by frequent glances in the small mirror which he had pasted to the inside cover of one of his reference books, referring to the mirror more often than to the book itself. These examinations satisfied him that all was well on the top of his head – a reassurance that kept his temperature down, which was important as when he sweated the hair curled until it looked like an upturned crab stranded on his skull.

As he sat there with no one consulting him, the Judge knew that there must be plenty of cases to be ruled on. He had served in towns like this all of his life at the bar, having resigned himself to the fact that he would never be selected for higher courts, and his considerable experience in delivering justice in such places told him that there were always petty squabbles to be sorted out. There was no more fertile territory for disputes than a moderately prosperous small town, where any improvement in wealth was immediately obvious, bringing with it envy and its sister sin of chicanery. This was why Judge Olin Prescott had paid no attention to the Police Sergeant's claims of harmony, preferring instead to watch Meabh Slevin run without looking where she was going in the disappointed hope that she would hit something. Harmony and a town like this were incompatible as likely to coexist as he was to have a case to hear that day, so he watched the clock tick by, having decided in advance that he would wait until 12.30 before packing his bags and leaving.

Outside the hall Judge Olin Prescott found that his appearance led to an instant clearing of the street. There had been about twenty people on the pavements, but one by one, as soon as they saw him, they all disappeared and in fifteen seconds only the dogs remained outside – and he sensed that even they felt uncomfortable about his presence. He walked to his car and left his bags in it before locking it again and setting off briskly in the direction of the house of Linus Gaynor. There he found about twenty people standing on the concrete path, huddled together to protect themselves from the chill east wind. The gable wall where they stood faced mostly north and so they could not stand in the rays of the low sun.

The Judge could not help but feel contempt for them. He knew that they were demented for the most part and at an earlier time in his life he would have found it in his heart to pity them – but not any more. This was no longer the same Olin Prescott who for his first ten years as a young barrister had worked at rates which were affordable to the poor. He had been an eloquent speaker then, capable of turning guilt into innocence so that those who could not pay their taxes would not go to prison for it. It was in those days that he had met his wife. Although of rich parentage herself, she could not but be impressed by his conviction that the law must always, always, side with the poor, even if they had broken it. Had that young barrister passed this way, there is no doubt that he would have looked upon the shivering pilgrims with angry compassion, but not so the judge he became. That Olin Prescott had lost his passion in the attricious years of ineffective jurisprudence. Despite his best efforts, he and those like him had never managed to make any impression beyond

obtaining the occasional exercise of a grudging clem-
ency or the overturning of a verdict which should
never have required such remedying in the first place.
Nor had they managed to give the lie to the hegemo-
nous charade that a rich man was never guilty. Down
through those long cumbersome years, the sense of
justice which had driven the young Olin Prescott
became entangled in the tentacles of the law, suffocating beneath the mounds of paperwork in anonymous
clerks' offices and in the endless periods of judicial
reflection until it died completely, leaving behind a
fossil of itself in the shape of a man who now cared
more about procedure than efficacy.

That he had become so cynical did not dismay him
any more. He had already gone through that stage and
had now progressed to the phase of his life when his
cynicism was at its most impressive as it had power to
go with it. He did not consider this phase to be his final
one, however, for he believed most earnestly that
before he died he would emerge from it to become a
more considerate man and spend his last days contemplating the paradox of a career which had begun with
such good intentions but had reached maturity in the
company of disillusionment. That day would come he
did feel, and for the sake of his soul he knew it had
better. But for now he continued to live the penultimate
phase, curling up the side of his mouth as he watched
the forlorn group standing in the cold staring up at the
window of Linus Gaynor like a job lot of expectant
Romeos. 'If he ever walks on water for them it will
certainly be the Last Day,' he thought to himself, 'and
we will all be rid of this.'

When he had seen as much as he was prepared to
withstand, Judge Olin Prescott walked round to the
front of the house. This was no longer the riot of colour

which it had been in the days when Gretchen Gaynor spent every daylight hour pandering to her flowers. The front door was closed, but the Judge had been told that Linus Gaynor was never left alone so he knew that there would be someone inside to answer if he knocked. He pushed open the gate, which squeaked for oil, and took the few steps to the door.

Judge Olin Prescott started knocking, unconsciously launching into the tattoo he used when calling a court to order with his gavel – one tap, followed by two in quick succession, followed by a final tap. But before he could complete this sequence – before he even managed to hit the second of the two close knocks – the front door was open and he was staring into the face of Gretchen Gaynor. She had been waiting for the Judge for much of the morning. Her intuition had told her that he would not repeat his inobtrusive visit of two weeks ago, and as soon as she had completed the pickling of her onions she had placed a seat by her front window and sat there waiting for him.

'Good morning, Madam,' said Judge Olin Prescott bowing his head slightly.

'Good *afternoon*, Judge,' she replied. 'What can I do for you?'

Her confidence in correcting his error came as a surprise to the Judge, who was used to being treated with sycophantic reverence wherever he went. 'I wonder if I might have a word with your husband,' he said.

Gretchen Gaynor waited for a moment, continuing to look the Judge in the face. Her air of being uncertain whether to grant his request was in fact nothing but a sham: she had no intention of refusing, but she thought she would try to unsettle him before she let him enter, for it would serve her husband well to have the Judge

address him in a spirit of unease. Whether she succeeded in this was doubtful, but if nothing else it made
her feel better. After those few seconds she stood aside,
signalling with the merest tilt of her head for the Judge
to enter. She instructed him to remain at the bottom of
the stairs while she went up to her husband's bedroom
to announce his arrival, and returned some moments
later to the top of the stairs to call him up.

Gretchen Gaynor refused the Judge's request to be left
alone in the room with Linus, so he embarked on his
mission in her presence, standing at the end of the bed
and taking a small piece of paper from his pocket before
delivering a short speech. He began by warning Linus
Gaynor of the penalty for impersonating a judge. He
reminded him that there was only one rule of law, and
that he represented it in the town. He insisted that
Linus Gaynor stop his practice immediately, and intim-
ated that action would be taken against him if he did
not. The Judge observed that this would be a tragedy,
and that he had no wish to see Linus Gaynor in trouble
with the law – particularly since, as far as he could tell,
Linus Gaynor had dispensed excellent justice which
had stood the test of time. Indeed, the Judge had not
been able to uncover a single instance of a ruling
passed down by Linus being ignored or proving
unworkable. But that was not the issue. The question
was one of legitimacy, which was ultimately the only
foundation on which good law could be based, and
nothing that Linus Gaynor could decide, no matter
how correct it might be, could ever be legitimate. When
he had finished, there was complete silence in the
room, and the Judge seemed lost as to what to do next.
He was a man used to reactions to his rulings. Sometimes what he had to say provoked anger and despair,

sometimes joy and relief, but this time there was nothing, just the low gibbering of a lunatic outside the window. It was an atmosphere which made the Judge self-conscious and embarrassed, and he quickly made efforts to get away from it, nodding to Gretchen as if requesting to be escorted away. But she continued to sit apparently emotionless by her husband as she had throughout, stroking the hair above his forehead, and the Judge had to find his own way out.

They were not certain, but they thought they could sense from his hurried departure that the Judge had lost the encounter, defeated by the silence of the defendant and the knowledge that the legitimacy of any court he might establish would never enjoy the authority which sustained the rulings of Linus Gaynor. And they were correct in that supposition, for the Judge could feel no presentiments of victory as he walked away from Poule. As he strode towards the police station, Judge Olin Prescott knew that he was in for trouble ahead and that any tribunals he might preside over in the future would stand like impositions instead of justice.

When he had instructed the Police Sergeant to report any further judicial activities by Linus Gaynor, Judge Olin Prescott told the officer that he would return in one month and that he would then expect to have some cases to hear. It was his hope that these would involve the normal workload of a rural judge, but if that was not the case then they would consist of the prosecution of Linus Gaynor and all of those who assisted him in the act of law-breaking. 'Make no mistake about it, my friend,' said the Judge, 'you and I are going to put a stop to these kangaroo courts.' The Judge's inclusion of the Sergeant in his resolution did not make the officer of the law particularly happy, yet he had no choice but to feign acquiescence – which did not deceive the Judge for a moment. 'That's very kind of you, Your Honour,' said the Police Sergeant. 'I can hardly wait.'

Driving out of the town past the house of Linus Gaynor, Judge Olin Prescott saw that a larger crowd than before had gathered to chant at the window. The Judge could not prevent himself from shaking his head in dismay, then remembered to look in the mirror to check that his hair was still evenly distributed about his cranium and that no part of his skull was flamboyantly covered to the detriment of any other.

As he drove away, Judge Olin Prescott sensed that he was being watched by many pairs of eyes, and in the case of the ex-revolutionary Sydney Caulfield by a single eye. The same collection of eyes next saw Meabh Slevin running in the direction of Poule to enquire about what had happened. 'He's told us to put a stop to this,' said Gretchen Gaynor, 'or else we're all in trouble.' When she had been told this, Meabh Slevin ran off again, this time to spread the word that confrontation was now unavoidable. This was an errand which gave her immense satisfaction, as there was nothing pleased her more than delivering messages of impending conflict. It was a role she had grown accustomed to during the periods of armed conflict, when it was rare for a week to pass without her running about to holler the news of this atrocity or that. Like the time she brought word of the death of Larry Knocks during the civil war, the day which ended with the entire population being taken to the Farmers' Hall where they spent the night mourning at gunpoint the defenestration of a teenage stranger while in the custody of his enemies. Those periods had supplied endless opportunities for Meabh Slevin to engage in her favourite pastime, and now with another battle in sight she ran about like a cat who'd caught sight of the cream and found that her enthusiasm was undiminished.

It seemed that Meabh Slevin's predictions of trouble had little effect, however, for few of those who watched the car of Judge Olin Prescott disappear from sight were in any way inclined to heed his warning that there should be an end to the proceedings at Poule. It was not bravado which drove them to seek open conflict with the normal law: they simply felt that there was no question of the law being broken in the first place. What happened in the bedroom of Linus Gaynor was nothing more than the seeking of good advice from a source which was widely respected. In the years since he had begun to hand out judgements, Linus Gaynor had seen to it that order and right prevailed – a goal which the previous system had consistently failed to achieve. That they should throw away such stability at the insistence of a man they had never heard of until a few weeks before did not seem right to them, and so they gathered themselves together to select a delegation to go to Poule and ask Linus Gaynor to ignore Judge Olin Prescott. They were sure that something could be worked out. It might be that they would need to proceed with greater secrecy, or even put up imaginary cases for the Judge to hear when he paid his monthly visits, but they were unanimously against abandoning all of the good which had been done. Conscripted into this group rather than joining of his own volition was Police Sergeant Donald Kilgallon, who would take orders from whoever spoke to him last, so that the instructions of the Judge became secondary to those of the people as soon as the Judge's car disappeared from sight. He was instructed to disregard everything he saw at the house of Linus Gaynor. If he did so then there would be no need for him to worry, for preparations were already being made to concoct bogus disputes for the Judge to arbitrate on when he returned. 'That sounds like a marvellous idea,' he said. 'I can hardly wait.' To everyone involved, this appeared to be the perfect compromise, for no one would lose and, most importantly of all, it would allow Linus Gaynor to continue to administer intelligent justice well into the future.

To Gretchen Gaynor, the arrival of the delegation from the people was as predictable as that of the Judge. She felt the situation become a real burden for the first time. There had never been a time in her life when it had been her intention to break the law, and the words spoken by Judge Olin Prescott to her husband were the first words of admonishment she had ever heard directed at a member of her family from the legal establishment. Had circumstances been different she would have sent the people away and told them that the game was up. But her foremost thoughts as she sat listening to them unfold their considered plan were for her husband. Listening to the intrigue which now seemed necessary if they were to continue as before, she felt more acutely than ever an all-embracing sorrow for him. Circumstances had never really allowed her to reveal such an emotion before, for it seemed that there was no place for sorrow in the fight to keep Linus Gaynor alive. She had often wanted to mourn with him, to hold him in her arms and cry on his head for a day so that he would know that above all else, above all the sentiments of defiance, of wit, of confidence in the future, above all those things which were so necessary to keep going on, above all those things she felt more sorrow for him than anything else. It was an emotion which had become the ubiquitous silent partner of all her other feelings for him. It was there when

119

practicality wiped his arse, when compassion rubbed ointment on his bedsores, when patience changed his wet sheets – accompanying all of those things was a lurking sense of sorrow. Sometimes, indeed, she thought that he would be better off dead, though she always quickly followed this sentiment with a brisk sign of the cross to absolve herself of ever thinking such a thing.

Gretchen Gaynor knew that her husband would not last long without the constant stimulation which people brought him. She also knew that when they stopped coming his decline into death would be unimaginably pitiable. There would be nothing for him but a long silent exit, like a man drowning far away from anybody, unable to signal his plight and the terror which accompanied it. Only in his eyes would she be able to glimpse what he would feel in those days, and being truthful with herself she did not think she would have it in her to look into them day after day and see the man she loved slowly recede from her until even his eyes no longer conveyed a message. That, she felt, was not good enough for Linus Gaynor: someone who had been through what he had been through was entitled to more than that. So she conveyed the message of his blinking eyes to the delegation of the people and told them that if they wished him to continue then he would do so. With that, all seemed as happy as was possible under the circumstances.

Judge Olin Prescott had always known that his instructions would be met with almost total disobedience. On the few occasions on which he had met Police Sergeant Donald Kilgallon, nothing the officer of the law had done gave the Judge any reason to believe that he would be effectual in stopping the activities at Poule.

He also knew that the police officer would not go out of his way to gather intelligence on those who continued to visit Linus Gaynor in search of judgements. In effect, the Judge knew that what he had done and said that morning was nothing more than an early skirmish in what would prove a long battle to wrest the law from Linus Gaynor's bedroom. Being able to visit the town only once a month did not make it easy for him to fulfil the task which the Minister of Justice had set him, but that was beyond his control. Judges were none too plentiful at that time, for it was a continuing legacy of colonialism that to take a seat on the bench was to label oneself as suspect at best and as corrupt at worst. It was acceptable to be a barrister – indeed folklore was embroidered with many cases of righteous advocates – but once higher office was attained trust was replaced by empty respect and those who wore a judge's robes could expect no affection. In his circuit Judge Olin Prescott sat behind the most respectable furniture that could be found for him, administering justice in a mechanical way without receiving any affection in return. He always kept himself apart from the people so that he could observe them better, and from his vantage point he had been able to develop an understanding of them which was uncanny to those who did not practise his profession but simply inevitable from where he sat day after day. Though his two visits to the town had left him with no illusions about the difficulty of the task ahead of him, he knew that he had at least succeeded in returning the official law to the fray, and that whatever faced him on his return would be shaped by the knowledge that Linus Gaynor was no longer unchallenged in his position as the dispenser of wisdom. The acceptance of that would be the first sign that he was having an effect. It was a thought which gave him some satisfaction – as much as the sight of his well-behaved hair, which had obeyed his instructions meticulously in recent months, a fact he put down to his advancing years and the final exhaustion of his follicles.

His journey at last brought him to the outskirts of the capital, which he returned to every night with an indifference brought on by the lack of excitement in his life. It was many years since he had last admired the beauty of the city from a distance, particularly when it was approached from the south-west so that the mountains to the north rose up behind the buildings like a monster. In his earlier years he had often used that route when returning from an evening of courtship, and many a girl had seen the capital in a different light because of the eulogies paid to it by the then barrister Olin Prescott. He still could not fail to wax poetic in the summer twilight as he gazed at the city of his birth and saw in it the beauty that was rarely celebrated by its inhabitants except when they sang half-hearted eulogies to it after drinking too much alcohol. But it had been years since Judge Olin Prescott had noticed the cityscape at other times. Driving towards it on the evening of his encounter with Linus Gaynor, the Judge felt himself looking again at the magnificent place, the magical skyline and, most impressive of all, the mountains behind. He felt like the young man of old, gasping large breaths of air to accompany the view, and between his legs he could feel a stiffening which he had believed would never trouble him again except in the early mornings after he had drunk too much alcohol. It was like the laying on of the warm hand of Venus, and he found himself giggling with the excitement of a juvenile. 'It's the Resurrection,' he laughed to himself – 'the Easter of my fornication. Blessed be God.' When he could no longer drive with safety, he stopped and got out so he could give his sensations his undivided attention. He remained standing for half an hour as the last remnant of natural light went away, and then lingered on to watch the lighting up of the city. When it became too cold to remain and he continued his journey, he was filled with the desire to buy his wife some flowers – something he had not felt for twenty years. In delivering them he went to kiss her. When he put his face forward to deliver the present, she reeled back as if in fear. But he took hold of her head and gently kissed her lips, despite the tugging that was going on. It was not that she did not want to be kissed by him – she simply did not expect it. And his intentions caused her no end of confusion for the rest of the evening, for he made no comment which might explain his behaviour. Instead she occasionally caught him glancing at her with a wry smile on his face, and despite her enquiring what this was all about he said nothing to put her mind at rest. 'There was a time when you looked at me like that if I didn't kiss you,' he said to her. 'Cannot a man show affection for his wife without an inquisition?'

Chapter Six

Darius Gaynor had never found it easy to consider the fate which it seemed nature had ordained for the males who were born into his family or who joined it through marriage. Despite the obvious absence of elderly men when the family came together for funerals, no one ever considered it right to speak to the young men about this. Instead there was an unmentioned agreement that the passing of time would limit the ambitions of the growing males, as they each in turn became aware that none of their forefathers had managed to live beyond two score and fifteen. For many of them, the realising of their fate was greeted with nothing but contempt for their ancestors who had carried such ill-fortune down through the ages.

A tragic example of this resentment came only a week after the death of Urban Gaynor, who had been unusual in that he never bore any hatred against the men who went before him. Urban Gaynor's adult years had been marked by an unending series of conquests which he had set himself the task of achieving in the years allotted to him. From the age of seventeen, when it was presumed he first accepted the limited duration of his existence, Urban Gaynor had become excited by the most dangerous of activities. By his eighteenth birthday he had already dived a hundred times from the cliffs at Shinnock into the sea which lay fifty yards below. His mother had been so upset when she first heard of this that she locked him in his bedroom, only to see him leap from the window down in front of her as she stood in her kitchen washing parsnips. He ran off in the direction of the cliffs and dived head first over the edge without even stopping to remove his clothes.

By the time he was twenty Urban Gaynor had stopped jumping from the cliffs at Shinnock and had taken instead to wrestling with bulls. The object of the game was to rub their noses in the grass. It was on his return from one of these contests that Urban Gaynor learned of the death of his father, who had collapsed while carrying a bag of pig feed. (It was never discovered if the cause of death was a heart attack or the crush injuries inflicted by the cargo.) Urban Gaynor, it was noticed, did not show any particular signs of grief at this event. Despite his insistence that he was stricken by the loss, no one was able to convince themselves that this was so. On the day of the funeral, Urban Gaynor watched the coffin being lowered into the ground, stayed for a few moments to shake some hands but then disappeared from the crowd and was seen some minutes later walking to the fields. There he broke the neck of a bull in a joust and remained for hours by the carcass crying like a child with an intensity he had not shown for his own father.

In the years after this event, Urban Gaynor continued to test himself against the most arduous of challenges. He climbed the vertical faces of mountains without ropes, swam the widths of roaring rivers, ate rat poison, and even tied himself to a truck and had someone drive it for a hundred yards, pulling him along the street as he had seen done in a film. He did all of these things without receiving more than minor injuries, only to die of the pneumonia he contracted on the night he walked for an hour in the rain along the county border, straddling the middle of the road with his feet and yelling at the top of his intoxicated voice that he was such a man it took two counties to support him. Despite the fact that they had all attended such funerals dozens of times before, there seemed a special air of loss surrounding the procession which took Urban Gaynor from the church to the cemetery. Those who carried him took care with their steps so as to soften the journey, and the crowd was uniquely silent as they went home having put him in the ground.

Unlike his father, Stanislaus Gaynor had never been able to regard the inevitability of his fate with anything short of anger. At the moment that Urban Gaynor passed from the world, Stanislaus had been thrown into a pit of depression which was most stridently characterised by his extreme silence. People tried to speak to him but he would not acknowledge them. Any attempted conversations quickly deteriorated into monologues and were given up as a waste of time. Stanislaus Gaynor did not emerge from this warren until a fortnight after his father had been buried, when he confessed to his mother that he did not think he could live with the sentence that hung over him. He told her that it was he who had removed the flowers from Urban's grave and that the footprints which covered the fresh soil were his. Everyone who heard his confession took pity on the boy and tried to convince themselves that his actions had been grief in disguise. Just as they did not discuss their fate with the young boys, a general silence descended about this incident with no one wishing to say what they were all thinking, namely that Stanislaus Gaynor's actions were nothing short of desecration. The footprints went deep into the soil and must have been the result of jumping. The flowers had been found well away from the grave, not placed at the side but flung with some venom. But this was an understandable crime, and the evidence disappeared with the caretaker's hoe and a bed of new flowers planted by an anonymous gardener. However, a second cloud descended on the head of Stanislaus Gaynor, who was never again treated with the respect he had once enjoyed. For although his crime was understood, this understanding was never extended to absolute forgiveness, and few could ever meet him again without conjuring up as a backdrop to their conversations the vision of his moonlit funereal bedlam.

Stanislaus Gaynor's behaviour had come as a shock to Darius, who was ten years younger than he, but even at the age of eleven he was able to sense that something wrong had occurred but had been quietly hidden from the folklore of the family, like a mad relative. But Darius had always resisted the temptation to pass judgement on his cousin with the same determination which prevented him from giving much of his time to considering his destined lifespan. Instead, he had remained busy pursuing other things, interests which Linus Gaynor passed on to him – sport, alcohol and, increasingly as he reached his early twenties, the prosperity of his business which had begun to put good food on the table. But throughout most of those years he knew in himself that the good nature which others often commended him for was the product of a mental detour which forbade him from passing too close to the fact which lurked constantly in the back of his head. For many years this trick had satisfied him, and it had been responsible for a happy childhood and adolescence. But since the first days of his courtship of Roberta Staunton, the falsity of that evasion had begun to trouble him. He slowly became aware that the poison which had lain dormant in his brain for all those years had sprung to life and would threaten his sanity unless he could expel it with his attention.

Darius Gaynor knew that there was nothing to be gained from ignoring any longer the truth of his destiny and so he went to his mother to ask her to tell him about the men who had died, demanding from her the most minute details she was capable of providing. She tried to evade his questions by moving away from him, but the more she did so, the angrier she detected her son becoming. He accused her of misguided compliance with the devious tradition which forbade people from talking about the dead for anything but the few days following their demise, and even then the subject was to be spoken of in affected surprise that one so young had been cut down in the prime of life. But there was nothing Gretchen Gaynor would say to him to satisfy his craving for information. He recognised in her a genuine inability, as genuine as the colour of her skin, to speak about the great calamity which chronically befell the generations. It was as if her mouth was incapable of uttering any words on the subject, prevented by a linguistic impediment from expressing anything more than regret that things should be as they were. 'Don't ask me to speak about such things, Darius,' she said to him, 'unless you want to break my heart.'

Unable to convince his mother of his need to know more about the men who had died, Darius Gaynor went further out among his relatives to see if any of the old women would be willing to talk to him. The beginnings of his search were not hopeful. When he broached the subject with Mimi Geoghegan, who had married Linus Gaynor's younger brother, she accused him of skulduggery, coming to see her as he had not done for eight years, concealing his intentions beneath the lie of concern he initially explained as the reason for his visit, and then prying into a vulnerable old woman's most personal affairs having softened her up with the humour of his tongue. Mimi Geoghegan would say no more to him, and only the weakness of her limbs stopped her from throwing him out of her house. Darius left her spitting invective at him from her door, and the half-empty cup of tea and the slice of currant cake with his teethmarks in it were both dispatched to the dustbin with the haste of a furious woman. But Darius was not daunted by this rejection. He told himself it had probably been a mistake to go to Mimi Geoghegan, for, as her name suggested, she had not waited long after the death of her husband before announcing that she wished to be addressed by her maiden name again. This reversion smacked of acute callousness to her husband's family, none of whom could ever bring themselves to utter her original name, and so she became known simply as Mimi – the woman whose pedigree was not to be mentioned.

He did not have much more luck with Linus Gaynor's sister Mona. She was less strident in her objections, but still felt that it was not a topic which she wished to discuss. 'You have to understand,' she said to him, 'that people don't think it right to mention these things. It is as if to talk about them will only initiate another episode. There is an understanding that everyone knows what everyone else is thinking. That is enough – there has never seemed a need to go any further.' This was what Darius Gaynor heard time and again from the old women – even from Florence Bean

Uí Carthaigh, who had mourned her husband Francis Xavier with a verve bordering on the distasteful. On the day of his funeral she had roared with such intensity that the larks left the cemetery and did not return for a month. Father Raymond Curtis had had his prayers continually interrupted by the screams of the woman, who let it be known to all who were there, and by the volume of her dirge even to those who were not there, that she could not go on without Francis Xavier. 'Not in a million years,' she yelled. 'Not if I inherited the earth. Not if you made me a child again. None of those things would make me able to go on without Francis Xavier. Not in a million years.' Above the noise of her lament, Father Raymond Curtis managed to complete his last words and the coffin was quickly lowered in the hope that its covering might quieten Florence Bean Uí Carthaigh. But there was to be no such luck and she remained for two hours in the same spot, long after her most loyal wailers had left because of the cold, until she had roared herself hoarse and the world could no longer hear the depth of her grief. Even Florence Bean Uí Carthaigh could not bring herself to speak to Darius Gaynor about the men. 'There is no end to it,' she said to him with the resignation of a woman who had herself searched for an answer but found none. 'There is no end to it, and talk is just a waste of time.'

Confronted by such a wall of silence, Darius Gaynor had no alternative but to abandon his search for someone to talk to. The more of the old women he went to see, the more they were expecting him and had prepared their reasons for refusing to discuss the matter. Dejected more than embittered, he went to the room where Linus Gaynor lay alone. Sitting with the old man, Darius remembered the days they had spent together when he was a boy. It made him laugh to think of the erroneous tips which his father had given him on the various crafts he believed every man should know, hints which Darius had found to be almost unanimously incorrect. It saddened him that he could not speak to the man without resorting to the blinking semaphore which would never prove adequate for the kind of conversation he wanted to have with him. Now in his middle twenties, Darius Gaynor wanted more than anything else to talk to his father. From the ruins of the conversations he had had in the previous days with the old women, he had gleaned that they were all in awe of Linus Gaynor for the blessing which had been bestowed on him. Darius was left in no doubt that his father's survival was now considered in celestial terms, a benediction which they all felt drawn to. Linus Gaynor had assumed the role of ubiquitous male in their lives, and secretly, in the privacy of their houses with the curtains drawn, they all considered him as theirs. That in the midst of the annihilation of their men one should survive, albeit in such a form, left them with bitter-sweet feelings. What it was about Linus Gaynor which had marked him as different they could not say, but they received his elevation with silent acceptance, loving him for the life that was still in him but not being able to see him without remembering all of those whose departure had made his survival so remarkable.

Sitting with his father, Darius was more than ever conscious of the limit placed on the time he had left. In many ways Linus Gaynor's survival threw the frailty of the other men into too stark a relief, and the longer he lived the more fragile they all seemed to be. Within ten years, Darius thought to himself, the next generation would begin to die. If Linus Gaynor was still alive then, there would be another set of widows who would look upon him with that mixture of religion and envy in the privacy of their houses. Darius reckoned that he was now about halfway through his life. With the love he had for Roberta Staunton he felt it deep inside him that she might well be one of those women who would grow old alone and before their time, and, worst of all for her, feeling embittered that her husband was gone while his father continued to lie alive in state. Darius kissed the old man on the forehead and left the room to go to his bed.

Despite the intensity of his love for Roberta Staunton, which seemed to prosper with every passing month, Darius Gaynor had never mentioned to her the fate of the men in his family. He knew that there would come a time when to delay its revelation any longer would be a terrible act of secrecy and that they were fast approaching that day. The days of their simple love between midday and one o'clock now seemed so remote that they could have been passages from the history of another man. The effects of the intervening period had changed them both from shy sweethearts at lunch-time into partners in a romance which equalled anything they saw at the cinemas on Friday and Saturday nights where they swam in the lightness of touch that only young lovers can summon. As Darius had watched Roberta Staunton emerge from the room of her past, he often could not but congratulate himself on the success of his persistence which he believed was all that had saved her from a life of permanent bitter reflection. That, he was sure, would have been a tragedy, for the more he knew her the more he saw the warmth that she was capable of. He wanted to wait until he was sure she was well away from her feelings of bitterness before he told her of the fate which he had long since accepted as inevitable for him. Only when he was certain that she would not begin again to damn

the cusp of Aries on which she was born for the ill-
fortune it chronically brought her did he feel it safe to
alter their plans to go to the cinema and instead took
her down along the quays where they had not walked
since their lunch-times of naïve affection, hoping that
they would remind her of her emergence from bitterness, the part of the world where she had recovered her
potential for love.

He had decided beforehand that there was no way to
shape the truth to make it any more palatable. There
was nothing he could say that would lead to anything
other than the inevitability of his early demise. So he
did not decorate the story with superfluous bunting,
but told her straight out of the deaths of so many of his
male relatives. He told her of Eamonn Denis Otis, who
had departed at the age of fifty-three while darning his
socks. Of Iggy Padraig Philip, who died while receiving
the sacrament of confession, falling into the aisle of the
church with a thud which woke the tramp sleeping on
the second-last bench. Of James Mary Oliver, who
collapsed just after buying a new pair of brown leather
shoes. These had been his first purchase of brogues in
over twenty years, and it was suspected that the excitement had been too much for his heart. Of Vincent
Gregory Samuel Arthur, who had written his epitaph at ·
the same time that he wrote his will, the occasion being
the first night of his marriage, when he was twenty-
three. Stored in the vault of a bank along with his most
important documents, it was not to be read for another
twenty-six years. Then, when he had died, its contents
displayed an all too accurate prescience: 'Here lies
Vincent Gregory Samuel Arthur Gaynor, who lived for
about fifty years but would not have said "No" to
another score.' The list went on for another half a dozen
until Roberta Staunton told Darius that he could stop:

she had heard enough. But he insisted she hadn't, for he had yet to tell her of his own father, Linus Gaynor, who at that very moment was lying as he had done for many years.

Roberta Staunton told him that she did not care about any of these things. She repeated the sentiments that he imagined had been uttered time and again through the generations when the reality of the curse was revealed, sentiments full of the confidence of youth with the prospect of many years together ahead of them. 'It would be worth it,' she said to him, 'to live together for twenty-five years no matter what the eventual outcome.'

'But what will happen to you when I'm gone?' he said to her. 'I don't want you to become like the other women, unwilling to talk about the truth and turning questioners away like they were tax-collectors.'

But she stopped him from speaking any further. 'Darius, there was a time in my life when I was prepared to hide the truth inside me and I almost died from its poison,' she said. 'I promise you I will not behave like that any more.' She promised him that she would not retreat to a solitude behind her curtains, venturing out only when summoned to another funeral. 'No, Darius,' she insisted to him – 'never again, never again. I will not live like that any more.'

The day that Darius Gaynor had set aside to ask Roberta Staunton if she would consent to be his wife was filled with potential from the point in the morning when he was woken by the alarm clock which Sylvester Bermingham, brother of Milo, had given him on the occasion of his twenty-first birthday. With all the hypocrisy of a hypocrite, Sylvester Bermingham had placed the box in the hands of the young Darius Gaynor accompanied by the foolish words that no man should ever wake after eight in the morning. In fact Sylvester Bermingham himself had not seen the sight of a morning since the last day of his school years, and he was now forty-four. He had concealed his hatred for the alarm clock beneath the lie of camaraderie, telling Darius Gaynor that he could think of no one he would prefer to have the family heirloom than he, passing it on as a player does the gun in Russian roulette, for despite the fact that he never wound the timepiece, Sylvester Bermingham's mornings were always filled with anxiety that the clock might ring out one last chime in anger at its being ignored for so long. Only in the hands of Darius Gaynor had it fulfilled its intended role, waking him at half past five every morning just as it did on the day he had decided to ask Roberta Staunton to marry him. While he had been eating his lunch that day, which consisted of sandwiches, which he liked for their efficiency, he had seen something which made him feel as sad as it made him feel lucky. He saw a man in the infancy of poverty introducing himself to the tramps who sat near the ferry gates, his clothes newly soiled by what Darius Gaynor guessed had been the first few days without a roof over his head.

In the evening, the thought of seeing Roberta Staunton again made his insides quake with excitement. Since the days when they had restricted themselves to a limited companionship, he had grown to love her beyond anything else in the world and he knew that something had taken root inside him which he could not stop growing: that for the rest of his life he would love Roberta Staunton with a ferocity which would take him to violence in defence of his passion if need be. When he asked her, she replied 'Yes' before he had finished speaking, and he promised her that he would not allow anything to separate them. With that he placed on her finger a ring which had taken him a week of transporting kale to buy.

When they drove to Poule that night there was a thick fog descended over the countryside. It was Hallowe'en, and as they passed the houses and the small towns on the way, the streets were lined with bonfires and the whole country looked like something from pagan times. Roberta Staunton counted over fifty fires before she gave up, and still they passed more, with dancers leaping about in front of them like grotesque goblins in a frenzy of celebration. Things were no different as they approached Poule. Darius Gaynor was able to point to the light around which he knew Milo Bermingham would have gathered with his brothers to drink alcohol and play music, cavorting in a way which many people believed to be silly given their ages, the youngest of them, Austin, being now thirty-eight. Above the concrete where the pilgrims had stood during the day, ignoring as they always did the bitter cold and the rain, there was a faint light from the room of Linus Gaynor. There Darius expected to find his mother reading to her husband from the newspaper or from a book if he had blinked in annoyance at the thought of having to listen to the news of politics which was all the papers seemed to carry any more. Darius Gaynor led Roberta Staunton to the door of the house, ignoring the shouts of Cecil Bermingham, the corrupt councillor, to come and dance with them by the bonfire. From the hall he could hear his mother's voice murmuring in the bedroom at the top of the stairs, so he led Roberta Staunton up to the room, clinging to her hand as they went. When she saw them standing at the door of the bedroom, Gretchen Gaynor put her book down on her lap and smiled at them both, for she had not seen them together for some time, but the nervous look on the young woman's face told Gretchen that they had come on a matter of importance and she could not think to herself that it could be anything other than to announce that they were to be married.

Gretchen Gaynor was correct in her assumption. Darius did not spend any time on preliminaries but announced their decision before Roberta Staunton even had time to close the door behind her. Gretchen Gaynor did not know what to say. She instantly remembered the time she had been introduced as a prospective bride and the words she had been given by Linus Gaynor's mother about the inevitability of things. All through her motherhood she had known that there would come a time when she would have to say the same thing for the first time, but she did not feel ready to do it yet. She could not find it in herself to feel enthusiasm for the news. Though she desperately wanted to be happy for them, Gretchen Gaynor was filled with foreboding and she did not like the prospect that awaited them. But happiness had not lately been the rule of things when such news was announced. It had long since been replaced by practicality and, it must be said, honesty. So Gretchen Gaynor rose from her chair and crossed to where her son and Roberta Staunton were standing. In her eyes they could tell what she felt, and it was no more or less than they imagined she would feel, for to accept the news as she had done was proof of her compassion. The three of them stood with arms around each other, and Gretchen whispered into Roberta Staunton's ear that they should talk together before the night was over as there was an honoured ritual to be gone through.

When Gretchen Gaynor had finished hugging her son and Roberta Staunton, the three of them turned to face Linus Gaynor. They all became aware that the room was too silent. Even by the standards of silence of which he was capable, Linus Gaynor was quieter than they had ever known him. It was not that he was making any less sound than was usual, as he was incapable of any sound at all, but the silence which had descended on the four of them came from the lack of something other than noise. Linus Gaynor lay looking at the ceiling, his eyes motionless as the three stared at him, moving closer as if by some signal from the wings, homing in on his face until they surrounded it. Not a word was spoken, but when they were very close to him he began to blink his eyes twice in quick succession.

Through all of his years of exercising them, his eyelids had developed muscles which were stronger than normal – so strong that the ferocity with which he now blinked made a sound, two taps in quick succession, warning them that Linus Gaynor would not have this, that he was not prepared to consent to the marriage. Darius Gaynor was numbed by his father's refusal. This was the man he had loved so intensely all of his life; the man who had imparted so many unreliable skills during the long hours they spent together when Darius was a boy; the man that Darius had cared for since their roles had been reversed by his father's paralysis. And now, after all they had enjoyed and suffered together, his father was not prepared to consent to his marriage, lying instead with his eyelids tapping, a sound which temporarily halted the dancing at the Berminghams' bonfire when they stopped to try to discover the source of such an unusual noise.

In the days which followed, Gretchen Gaynor could do nothing but try to persuade her husband to tell them why he was so outraged at the idea that his son should marry, but she was unable to squeeze a reason from him. Despite the intensity of her pleading, during which she told him that Darius Gaynor would never forgive him if he did not change his mind, Linus Gaynor remained unwilling to reveal the reason for his intransigence, and so he left his wife for the first time with the feeling that she was married to a selfish man. Gretchen Gaynor could imagine no reason for her husband's behaviour other than that he did not want anything to change, that he saw Darius Gaynor's becoming a husband as a potential threat to the dominance of Linus Gaynor, who had paid such a high price for his status and did not feel that anyone was entitled to usurp his position. In sessions of screaming frustration, Gretchen Gaynor yelled this at her husband so loudly that the lunatics outside became accustomed to it and laughed when it happened.

Through the window of his room, it became known to everyone that Linus Gaynor would not consent to the marriage of his son. Such was Linus Gaynor's sway over people that Darius began to receive anonymous messages of advice which soon became messages full of innuendo and eventually of hate. They told him that what his father had decided should be obeyed. Just as everyone else was prepared to abide by his judgements so too should his son, for there could, they said, be no more despicable form of treachery than Darius Gaynor refusing to heed what his father had ruled. But in spite of the nameless insults which were written – for no one had yet had the courage to stand before him and shout such bile into his face – Darius Gaynor could not obey his father. He had never imagined that they would ever argue with such feeling. He often found it difficult to believe that they were moving apart at a speed which would shortly take them all of the way to hatred. When the possibility of such animosity became too real for him, he would have to prevent himself from thinking about it any longer by doing something to distract his attention. But that was never easy, and many were the times he had had to halt his van by the side of the road because he could not see for the tears in his eyes.

Chapter Seven

Had it not been for the size of his frame, Father Raymond Curtis might, given a suitable disguise, have managed to move among the people anonymously. But he was far too tall for that, his head being well over six feet from the ground, large and red like a disembowelled Hallowe'en pumpkin. There had never before been a time when he had regretted being so tall. His colossal height had made him a much sought-after rugby player, a demand contributed to by his ability to shield illegal blows to his opponents with his body and the severity of his tongue which cowered other teams into subservience. His dashing figure had brought him the constant attention of women, and he would tease them by delaying the revelation of his profession until they had flaunted themselves before him beyond doubt. He excused his behaviour as being nothing more than a natural sense of humour, and even when it seemed the temptations were more than any man could refuse, Father Raymond Curtis had never wavered from his chastity, for behind all of his flirtation he did truly believe that he had been born only to serve God and to play rugby, in that order.

In his younger years he had attended to his mission in rugby with admired diligence. Now that he was older and his body growing over instead of up, all of his attentions were concentrated on the service of God. He believed that this was best achieved by the campaigning zeal of a Samaritan, and so he spent much of his time with the poor and the dying, anointing the terminally ill with the same hands which had broken so many faces in the past. Like the hero from a fairy tale, he was a huge and powerful man whose hands the size of chairs were capable of the most delicate caress, and when the sick called for a priest to prepare them for death they always called for huge Father Raymond Curtis, who possessed in his touch the power to overcome their fear of decay.

The things which Father Raymond Curtis had seen in the course of his days had often made him an angry man. In his early years as a priest he had worked in the capital. There he was daily confronted by the spectre of economic failure in the sprawling tenements which grew without pause and all the time increasing the pressure on those who lived in them. In those burgeoning slums he was forever looking at failure. When he felt he could take no more and was in need of hope, he would cycle to one of the orphanages with a box of cabbages on his carrier. There at least, he could see the merest chance of a better future in the children, the younger of whom had been abandoned because of poverty, the older having lost their fathers and mothers to the bullets of intolerance during the terrible wars. The anger which Father Raymond Curtis felt was often taken on to the rugby pitch, where he was constantly listening for a certain accent which indicated wealth. If detected, this would condemn the bearer to an uncomfortable eighty minutes, if not a broken limb.

Father Raymond Curtis had never lied to the people, but told them that God was as much a part of the problem as He was a part of the answer. Such expression of religious anarchy inevitably drew his teaching to the attention of his superiors, and he received several messages carrying warnings about his heretical talk and insisting that he stick to vaguer monologues about the promise of better things to come. When he first received such a warning, he tried to obey it in deference to his superiors, but what he saw in response was a lessening of the anger among the people which he felt was essential to the improvement of their lot. 'Don't fall asleep in your poverty,' he would say to them – 'wake up to its brutality. See it for the demon that it is.' Subservience was no substitute for directed anger he concluded to himself, and he returned again to the kind of talk which had earned him the reputation of a Catholic communist.

It was this reputation which eventually, after five years, led to his banishment. 'Send him away from the city,' said the Bishop. 'Send him out to pastor among the cattle and the vegetables.' And so Father Raymond Curtis received his marching orders from the capital, being seen to the city boundary like a medieval scoundrel. But though he was out of sight of his superiors from that point on, he was not out of sight of the people, his huge black figure moving about like the great bull of mythology, seeking out those who needed help, for Father Raymond Curtis had no doubt that even in the rural plains of honey there was poverty and sickness and he sought them out with an enthusiasm equal to that which had led to his exile from his native city.

When he first arrived, no one had ever seen anyone as big as him. Even the farmers who prided themselves on their magnitude looked small in comparison to him, and it came as a surprise that a man so powerful could possess such religious conviction. One of his first actions on arrival was to seek to raise the tops of the doors in his presbytery. He consulted Aongus Bermingham the builder, and brother of Milo the violinist, to see if this would be possible. But Aongus Bermingham insisted that the old building would not stand up to such rearrangement and offered the solution of lowering the floors instead. This appeared a satisfactory compromise, and so Aongus Bermingham set about digging a trench in each of the doorways. These were later to cause the retirement of Phyllis Murnaghan the housekeeper, who insisted that after fifty years' service the new doorways were more than her short legs could manage. Lowering the thresholds was the only comfort which Father Raymond Curtis granted himself, and he did it purely for medical reasons, for he was concerned that if he continued to bash his forehead against the tops of doorways he would end up in old age like the punchdrunk boxers who shuffled around the tenements in the capital and suffered the catcalls of the juveniles who dubbed them 'zombies'. So that he would not be open to any charge of misappropriation of funds, Father Raymond Curtis paid for the alterations from his own pocket. When the job was finished he spent over an hour wandering through his house without concern for his head, which was now free from the threat of bruising at least during the time he spent at home.

When he had satisfied himself that his head was as protected as was possible for a man of his size, Father Raymond Curtis set out one morning to find those things which needed remedying. He took his bicycle with him as it was the only method of transport he could use with any comfort. Motor cars were of no use as he had too much difficulty getting into them and even more difficulty getting out. It was only on his bicycle that he could travel, his knees pointing out in opposite directions and his big fists clasping the handlebars until they looked as if they might bend with the force. On his first morning Father Raymond Curtis had been awestruck by the beauty of the place. He had rarely seen such loveliness and could not help but contrast it with the decay of the capital, where it was impossible even to fill your lungs with clean air. In those first few days he looked like a phantom winging its way about, shouting greetings to anyone he passed.

Meabh Slevin was one of the first to see him. She was running back to her house to micturate, as the damp weather always made her want to go, when she observed the great black figure pedalling towards her, his knees spread out so wide it was impossible for anything to pass him on the road. In that bellowing voice which was to become so well known in time, he roared at her that it was a wonderful day if somewhat cold, and the noise of his voice brought several people out on to their front steps to see what was causing such a commotion. 'I thought another war had broken out,' said Cormac Sheehy-Skeffington. 'His voice was so loud I was sure it belonged to an ambitious colonel, like the ones who used to descend on us regularly and call us all into the streets to instruct us as to which side we were on this time.' Cormac Sheehy-Skeffington was not alone in the belief that Father Raymond Curtis's volcanic voice signalled the beginning of another war. Una Aine Nora Balfe had read sinister implications into her cats' disappearing beneath the piano which stood in her living-room, for the start of the two previous wars had been signalled by the animals detecting in the yells from the street the arrival of another bunch of hoodlums who measured terror in decibels and filled .

everyone's heads with the din of their concocted military jingoism. After she discovered the cause of the rumpus that morning, it took Una Aine Nora Balfe another two weeks to coax all of her animals from under the piano, the creatures surrendering individually, and the last of them abandoning its refuge only after Donncha Balfe had played 'The Bluebells of Scotland' sixteen times in ten minutes.

It was probably the relief that so many people felt when they discovered the true cause of the noise that morning that made Father Raymond Curtis become so instantly popular. Within weeks of his arrival he had been confided in on the most personal matters, his confessional becoming as much a site of counselling as of absolution. In his box he learned of the true state of things, the events which were concealed beneath that beautiful rural carpet and which were aired only when their perpetrators were in the presence of the enormous man of God. Sitting at right angles to his confessors, Father Raymond Curtis began to hear of the stories which were eventually to lead to the adoption of Linus Gaynor as judge and eventual saviour. He caught glimpses of the circumstances which allowed for the evolution of such a figure: the chronic alcoholism, the brutality, the poverty, the hunger, the bitterness, the envy – and all of these without any redress from the law. So it came as no surprise to him when he first heard that people were visiting Linus Gaynor to ask for judgements on matters of dispute.

Father Raymond Curtis had first heard of the court of Linus Gaynor from Evelyn Fitzpatrick on one of the occasions when he had been hoodwinked into visiting her in the belief that she was too seriously ill to attend mass. A young messenger had been sent to the priest with a slip of paper on which she had scribbled a barely

legible note (Evelyn Fitzpatrick was an excellent calli-
grapher) that she wished to receive Holy Communion
and would the priest come to her house that Sunday
afternoon to administer the sacrament? This he had
done gladly, relinquishing the spare hour he normally
kept for doing his 100 Wagner-accompanied press-ups
in his bedroom. When he arrived at her house, Father
Raymond Curtis had been astonished to find the
author of the letter in high spirits. She told him that she
had undergone a remarkable recovery, so complete
that she had spent the morning in her kitchen baking
soda bread. In all, he was detained for over two hours
that day, during which he not only had to entertain her
dull conversation but was also forced to eat the dreadful bread, which had him flatulating profusely for
several hours afterwards.

The only compensation of the visit was that it had
been Evelyn Fitzpatrick who told him first that people
had begun to visit the house of Linus Gaynor in search
of justice. Although he had been disillusioned by what
he had heard of the behaviour of the judges who came
to the town, he was a little sceptical when he first
heard this story. As it came from Evelyn Fitzpatrick, a
woman who he had ample evidence was not averse to
lying, he was inclined to take her description of the
activities at Linus Gaynor's house with the same doubt
with which he received her subsequent messages of
ill-health, but he was still sufficiently aware of the lack
of belief in official justice not to dismiss her story without investigating it for himself.

When he left the house of Evelyn Fitzpatrick he did
not go straight to Poule in case the deceitful woman's
story was a fabrication, in which case he would have
felt a fool. Instead he carried out a more surreptitious

study, establishing a miniature observatory in his bed-room with the help of a pair of binoculars from the Boer War (or so the antique dealer assured him) and a mirror hung from the handle of his window. By this means Father Raymond Curtis was able to see the front door of Linus Gaynor's house while appearing to look in the opposite direction, and it took him no more than an hour to confirm the story which he had first heard in the course of sampling Evelyn Fitzpatrick's damaging soda bread.

In many ways Father Raymond Curtis had been pleased at the confirmation of the story. In his time in the capital he had seen every day the disastrous conse-quences of unrespected law. That the citizens of the town had managed to establish an effective system of justice was to their credit. He had no idea of how long it might last, but in the absence of anything more substantial he was sure that nothing harmful would come of it. With such a feeling he was able to visit Linus Gaynor regularly without any sense of conniving with a charlatan. Indeed he sensed that his visits provided the additional spiritual legitimacy which people were looking for, which pleased him as he had not heard of any rulings handed down by Linus Gaynor which had not been considered to be wholly correct.

For as long as Linus Gaynor continued merely to preside over matters of the law, Father Raymond Curtis remained ambivalent. Every day the priest could see the beneficial effects of the paraplegic's judgements, and he was able to discern a definite improvement in the quality of people's lives. He was not alone in this feeling. Many of those who came to see him on matters of religion informed him of the air of calm which had descended in the wake of Linus Gaynor's decisions. The older women spoke of how the slide into anarchy had been halted. For the young men, Linus Gaynor had become a father figure to whom they could look for guidance in the absence of their own fathers. This, the old women concluded, was one of his most important functions, for he instilled a new sentiment of respect among the young men, many of whom had grown violent for the want of discipline. The more of this kind of talk that Father Raymond Curtis heard, the more he grew to like Linus Gaynor as he saw in the man a fellow spirit of organised dissent. So when Father Raymond Curtis went to rub wine on the lips of Linus Gaynor, he privately thanked God for having such a blessing.

Father Raymond Curtis had long since been aware that everything seemed to happen in winter, and in early winter to be more precise. During his life he was to look back on many events which had happened at such a time and had brought about fundamental changes in the direction of his being. He had been born in early November, and he was always to regard this as important not just because his birth had been a necessary preliminary for the rest of his life, but also because the date made him a Scorpio, a birth sign whose characteristics he had always been conscious to live up to. It was not that he openly practised astrology, in fact he publicly sneered at anyone who did, but he secretly harboured the suspicion that there was something to it, but only in the case of Scorpios, which he regarded as the aristocrats of the stars. The major events of his life were to reinforce his suspicion that his birth sign was more significant than the rantings of a bothered gypsy, as they happened time and again during the reign of Scorpio in the early winter. His birth, his first confession, his confirmation, his ordination, his first view of the slums in the capital, all of these things happened

149

to him in the early winter, and it was in early winter that he first heard the news that Grainne Dearvla Feherty had been cured of her elegance and was running about with her story of a miracle at the hands of Linus Gaynor.

Father Raymond Curtis had not been in the town when the news had first begun to circulate. It was the morning after the clocks went back one hour and he had been called by the police to administer extreme unction to a pauper who had killed himself with rage when the reversal of time doomed him to an extra hour of poverty. It was perhaps the priest's fatigue at the time of hearing about Grainne Dearvla Feherty which prevented him from acting as he surely would have done if the circumstances had been different. It was half past eleven in the morning when Meabh Slevin ran to his house with the news. Father Raymond Curtis had been up since three o'clock that morning and was missing the sleep which he always needed to function properly. When Meabh Slevin told him the news, he had received it with nothing more than a cursory nod of his head, expecting that everything would go away in a short time. This had been a fatal error. Looking back at his inadequate response, he knew that had he not been suffering such exhaustion he would have gone straight to the house of the cured woman and insisted that she stop talking such nonsense as there were more pressing matters to be dealt with than trumped-up miracles which only ever served to distract attention from seeking real solutions to problems such as why a man had killed himself because of a trick of time. Had he done so, things might have been very different for Father Raymond Curtis, but then it was early winter and so it was time for important events to take place in his life.

As things were to turn out, by the time Father Raymond Curtis had realised the seriousness of what was happening, there was nothing he could do to stop it. He went to bed and snored his face off, but while he was doing so the news that Grainne Dearvla Feherty had been cured of her elegance grew from a tale among a few into a story worth the attention of the newspapers. They sent correspondents to see for themselves that this woman could now speak to people, a gift they reported with practised hyperbole accompanied by pictures of the face from which words could now flow in abundance and the window behind which lay in paralysis the source of her remedy. While all of this was happening, gigantic Father Raymond Curtis lay stealing back from the day the hours of sleep he had been denied in the night, so comatose that his slumber was not even broken by the knocking on his door as people tried to contact him to tell him about the curing of Grainne Dearvla Feherty.

By the time he had woken, the stories which would let the nation know that Grainne Dearvla Feherty was cured had been irrevocably committed to newsprint. The next morning Father Raymond Curtis received a thunderous telephone call from his Bishop demanding to know what he was going to do about the 'miracle'. Unprepared for the severity of the call, the priest reassured his superior that he would take care of it. But his promises were to be unfulfilled, as nothing on earth or in heaven could turn back the clocks twice in two days and Father Raymond Curtis became as much a victim of time as the man who had suspended himself from a roof because his sentence of poverty had been extended by one hour.

For every reason that there seemed possible to be, Father Raymond Curtis wished that he had not been born such a monstrous man. His most fervent wish from the day the clocks went back was to disappear beneath a cloak of anonymity to where he could hide the contempt which organised itself inside of him, spitting silent defamation at all those who believed that Linus Gaynor could work miracles and gathered at his wall like the faithful of Jerusalem with their hands clasped in deference and their eyes straining upward to his window. For Grainne Dearvla Feherty he reserved a special hatred and he would, if he could, have gagged her with one of his thickest socks until she agreed to revert to silence, although he had to content himself with expressing only faint enthusiasm, speaking merely of his wish that she would not have a relapse – a sentiment which he could not convince himself he really meant.

But the anonymity which Father Raymond Curtis so desired in those days was denied him by his size. It was impossible he found, even in the heart of the open countryside which still made him gasp with its beauty, for him to hide from the clamour for official approval which the new faithful demanded for the spiritual works of Linus Gaynor. Had he been short he could have disguised himself as a lunatic. He could even have hidden in the belly of that which he despised so much, mingling among the crowd beneath Linus Gaynor's window where no one would think to look for him. But now the height which had made him such an admired rugby player and the subject of so many unambiguous female advances was a curse, an indelible inheritance as unchangeable as if he no longer wished to be a Scorpio. What was most distressing for him was that he was confronted by believers even in those circles which he hoped would be unimpressed by the rumours. He found that the poor and the sick were as loud in their praise of Linus Gaynor as all of those who had the luxury of viewing his apparent gifts without the need for them to be their last hope of salvation. He could not distinguish the fervour of the dying from that of the healthy, or the fervour of the destitute from that of the rich. 'How could anything be more effective than having someone you know speaking directly to God?' they said to him.

'But it might all be a mistake,' pleaded Father Raymond Curtis. 'Don't ever underestimate your own ability to bring about change. Don't ever relieve yourself of that power.'

But despite his cautions that those in most need should not risk their cause by the fake protestations about this man's power taking the place of their own concerted action for change, Father Raymond Curtis found that his own message was not being heard any more above the arias of devotion which now rose up around Linus Gaynor. 'I am drowning at the height of the flood,' he wrote in his diary, 'and if I do not survive then who will there be to pick up the pieces once the waters have subsided?'

The most noticeable symptom of his loss of prestige was that no one listened to Father Raymond Curtis any more – unless he was eulogising about Linus Gaynor, that is, for when he spoke on that subject he found plenty of willing ears, but it was a terribly painful thing for him to do. Unable to lie low any longer he agreed to celebrate mass again in the bedroom of Linus Gaynor. He guessed that over 300 people came to pray, spreading themselves across the roads and ditches as they searched out vantage points. The priest had no alternative but to say some words about Linus Gaynor. He had never been a good actor, and all his life he had avoided their company because he was never sure if they would tell the truth. But on that day he acted to the best of his abilities, telling the crowd what they wanted to hear in as measured a tone as he could manage without raising suspicion. Everyone was prepared to listen to him on such an occasion, but when he later went to the poor and told them that they must organise themselves to extract better payments from the State, no one listened to him with anything more than courtesy, and from the involuntary nodding of their heads and the vacant looks in their eyes he could tell that they were not hearing him but their thoughts were on Linus Gaynor and what he might do for them if they prayed enough.

In addition to witnessing the collapse of rational thought in the town, Father Raymond Curtis had also to contend with the hostility of his Bishop. The two had never liked each other to begin with, and this fiasco gave the senior man the opportunity he had always wanted: a chance to vilify Father Raymond Curtis in the guise of trying to quell talk of a miracle. The Bishop had not been able to believe his luck when he first read of the events concerning Grainne Dearvla Feherty. He had roared with faked anger to impress upon his house staff that he was dismayed at yet another rumour of divine intervention, but in the privacy of his study he sniggered to himself and rubbed his hands round and round each other as he contemplated the possibilities which the incident presented him for chastising his unruly charge. He would avail himself of every means to impress upon Father Raymond Curtis the extent of his rage that such a rumour had been allowed to see the light of day. His explicit instructions that such talk was to be killed at birth had been ignored and now it was up to the priest to undo the damage which had flourished while he lay asleep during working hours. The Bishop called for a report from his subordinate. He dispatched his most ruthless servants to question Father Raymond Curtis, who was fully aware of the reasons behind the official chastisement he was suffering. The incident provided the perfect screen behind which to settle more personal scores, but there was nothing Father Raymond Curtis could do to expose the truth. To even try to do so would lead him into even greater trouble and accusations of trying to shift the blame for his own mistakes on to an innocent colleague.

Behind the rage which his office sanctioned the Bishop enjoyed himself tremendously. He had seen it all before and was in no doubt that in time the whole circus would disappear, and if he had his way it would take Father Raymond Curtis with it. The contents of his diary were never published, but in his notes of that time a subordinate suggested that it must have contained the words 'I've truly got that communist now.'

Never before had Father Raymond Curtis felt so emasculated. He could not believe that he had been so soundly beaten by this. In the past he had always felt that the combination of his physique and the strength of his character made him invulnerable. This was why he had so willingly antagonised his superiors, who he was sure would not be able to counter his moral authority with references to books of religious protocol. He had seen more of the real life of people than any of those superiors, who had risen to their positions through the practice of blinkered sycophancy, ignoring as they were elevated to higher office the conditions which existed beneath them and which they refused to regard as a matter of religious concern. So they never accepted his practice of organising demonstrations against the sacking of workers or against the filth of the tenements in which the only things which prospered were the cockroaches which carried disease into every room they visited. Nor had they seen anything but pornography when he fed the ugliest of the whores who had become rheumatic harridans through years of fucking on damp mattresses and whose bodies no longer enticed the men from the streets. But they never made their disapproval too public, refusing to be drawn from their sets to where he could have hit them with the stick of his justified righteousness. Instead they preferred to lurk near the back walls of their hides, from where only the whites of their eyes told of their presence, and from where they sent out messages of caution through private channels so that only Father Raymond Curtis would know that they thought his behaviour was inappropriate for a man of his position.

When he had received such messages in the past, Father Raymond Curtis had greeted them with the same seriousness as he did the cartoons in the newspapers he read. He was satisfied that he had nothing to be ashamed of and that if it came to a head he would be able to defend his actions without difficulty. He was sure that the people he helped would rush to his assistance. A mass of character witnesses comprising the poor, the sick, the lonely, the whores, the old, the young, like an army of the people, would, he had always been sure, rise up to defend him against the petty accusations of his superiors. But the silence which now greeted him when he spoke to these very people about how they should not rely on stories of intercession left him with the lonely realisation that he would not be saved by them: that if he called on them to prove that he had not been wasting his time, as was alleged, they would not come.

Father Raymond Curtis was angered as much by their stupidity as by their treachery. There were times when he could not contain his anger, reverting to behaviour he had not displayed since his days on the rugby pitch when he would grab the testicles of his opponents in the confusion of the maul where it was impossible to follow the hand back to its owner. Not that he started to grab the balls of the poor, but he began to shout at people that they were being deluded if they thought a virtual cadaver could help save them. 'You have to come to your senses,' he insisted, 'just the way you did when I first told you how powerful you could be.'

But his tirades set the children crying and only made him less welcome than before, and he was turned away from doors which had once extended the warmest of welcomes. This was a process which reduced him to the role of priest and no more. His radicalness was no longer required, and people only whispered to him that he should say more masses for Linus Gaynor. After several months of this, Father Raymond Curtis admitted to himself that he was beaten by this thing. The only way he could stop it was to go to Linus Gaynor himself and ask him to make it clear to all of those who gathered beneath his window and travelled the country in his name that he did not want them to do so any more, and that rumours of his powers were nothing more than the fantasies of a reformed woman of elegance who had realised what any person of sanity would have done, that she could not go through life without speaking to people and expect to be happy.

When Father Raymond Curtis did bring himself to the room in which lay the source of his decline, he asked to be left alone with Linus Gaynor. Despite the fact that he had been in the bedroom before and had seen Linus Gaynor in his paralysed state on many occasions, Father Raymond Curtis could not remember the place as feeling so small or so quiet before. Indeed,

157

were it not for the seriousness of his mission he would have considered it a violation to break the peace of the place with his booming voice, but then it was that very aura that he had come to overthrow. He stood with his hands resting on the back of the chair provided for devotees and bent his back until he was looking down into the face of the man who had robbed him so deftly and rounded the sides of his mouth until it resembled the barrel of a gun. 'I don't know what you think you're doing,' he said with a voice whose bass tickled the balls of his feet. 'I don't know what you think you'll achieve by all of this, but you're messing with something you know nothing about. I can't believe that a man who has been through what you have could live with the know-ledge that he was fooling the most vulnerable of peo-ple, let alone encourage it by his silence. You should see them out there, standing in the rain in their innocence. This isn't right. You're making fools of them and they can't afford such a diversion.'

It was not that he expected Linus Gaynor to reply to him, but Father Raymond Curtis could tell from the passivity of Linus Gaynor's breathing that he felt no inclination to respond even if he could. The priest could not continue to look at such a face, so he stared instead at the yellowed weeping figs and jasmine wall-paper which had borne silent horticultural witness throughout the deviant years. 'There has been no mir-acle performed in this house,' said Father Raymond Curtis when he could again look at Linus Gaynor. 'The woman Grainne Dearvla Feherty was on the brink of insanity, but what drew her back was the realisation that no one can go through life without the company of others. That's not a miracle, Linus Gaynor; that's com-mon sense. If you want to know what a miracle is then I'll tell you. I'll tell you about a mother living in the slums of the capital who had no money to feed her children. And how she one day went into a grocery store and filled a box with vegetables and walked out again without paying because she had no money. Do you think that woman went to jail, Linus Gaynor? She did not. She did not go to jail because no one dared to press charges against a woman who finally had the courage to say "Enough is enough." The shopkeeper wouldn't press charges against her, and she herself felt no cause for repentance because she knew that God would not punish her for such an act. Now that is a miracle, Linus Gaynor. Not this stuff. Not the claims of a deluded woman like Grainne Dearvla Feherty. You've not given people hope, you've simply made them believe that they cannot save themselves, and in time they'll burn your effigy for it. You'll become infamous, Linus Gaynor. They'll remember you like they do Judas Iscariot. But maybe that's what you want – the fame of a heretic is better than no fame at all.'

Father Raymond Curtis walked to the door of the bedroom and placed his hand on the cold handle. 'I ask you again not to pervert your influence,' he said without turning to look behind him. 'You could make a great contribution to their lives, Linus. You could enrich them by your determination to stay alive. But you'll lose all of that with this homespun voodoo.'

On the concrete outside there were a dozen or so lunatics chanting among themselves with rosary beads placed in their hands by their minders. Father Raymond Curtis could only look in desolation at them. He could only do likewise as he passed the houses where he knew people lived in poverty and behind whose doors lay the sick. 'It has all come apart,' he wrote in his diary. 'This man has duped them all beyond their reason, and nothing I can say matters any more.'

Father Raymond Curtis had never felt so helpless as he did on the morning after he had gone to see Linus Gaynor and been received with silent contempt. That night he had had a terrible nightmare in which both of his parents died. It was not their dying that was terrible, for they were already deceased. His mother had died of tuberculosis during the height of an epidemic, when the disease was taking people by the score every day. He had been with her at the time and held her in his arms as she called for his father for the last time, her mind vacant of the fact that he had been killed sixteen years before in a ruinous uprising led by a schizophrenic revolutionary. What was so terrifying for Father Raymond Curtis when he relived their demise in his dreams was that it was the first time he had had to bear their loss on his own. In the past he had been supported by God and by his relatives, but now as he lay in his bed having been betrayed by his certainties he could not find it in himself to do anything but weep at their loss. He did so for over an hour until the noise of the crows woke him from his grief.

In the dark-brown cabinet which stood in the study of the presbytery and which Father Raymond Curtis had always suspected of being mahogany, although he could not be sure as he did not know his woods terribly well, there were a number of whiskey bottles which had been standing like disciplined soldiers since they had been given to him by his closest friend Albert Costello-Davitt, who was an expert in soil mechanics. His knowledge took him around the world, and Father Raymond Curtis knew of no one who had sat so many times in an aeroplane and whose passport contained so many immigration stamps. Whenever he returned to see his close friend after one of his foreign trips, Albert Costello-Davitt, who was a professor in fact, would always bring a bottle of whiskey bought cheaply at an airport. He was aware that Father Raymond Curtis did not like whiskey, but he still insisted on buying it for him so that there would always be a plentiful supply when he came to visit. It was a habit which had become a tradition, and both of them would joke about it when a new bottle was produced – although it must be said that Albert Costello-Davitt laughed more than did Father Raymond Curtis. In all, six bottles now stood in the possibly mahogany cabinet. Father Raymond Curtis had never put his hand into it to pull out one of the bottles without being in the company of the professor of soil, but in the absence of anything else to calm him he did so that morning. He poured himself a glass of malt whiskey and took a mouthful which almost came straight back up and over his carpet, its passage only stopped by his slamming his mouth shut so the whiskey swilled around inside with nowhere to go until he gradually let it slip down into his stomach in manageable doses.

Father Raymond Curtis did not turn up for mass that morning. Those who had come remained for half an hour in the hope that he had been temporarily delayed, but then agreed that he was not going to appear and left in small groups muttering mild annoyance. Some of them were back that evening at half past seven, but Father Raymond Curtis did not arrive then either. This further absence was considered unacceptable, and so Meabh Slevin offered to run to the priest's house to see what was the matter. When she returned some minutes later, she was in a state of such excitement that Archie Bermingham, brother of Milo, knew immediately that there was gossip in her mouth. 'I'm very sorry to have to tell you this,' she lied, 'but Father Raymond Curtis is blind drunk in the presbytery.' Her words sent the congregation scurrying in the direction of the building where they gathered outside the front window and listened to the low murmuring sound of their priest singing 'The Little Red Fox' to himself.

There was nothing anyone could do to attract the priest's attention away from his music so that he would open the door and they could put him to bed and give him plenty of water to protect him from the hangover they knew he was due. Archie Bermingham was the most sympathetic, as he was a veteran of similar conditions. From where he stood outside the window, he was filled with such sympathy for the priest and the ordeal which was ahead of him that he blessed himself several times before leaving the rest of the audience to discuss the awful nature of Father Raymond Curtis's predicament. For another twenty minutes they tried their hands at lockpicking but without success, so in ones and twos they drifted away and for the rest of the evening those who passed the presbytery reported hearing Father Raymond Curtis still singing 'The Little Red Fox', his voice hanging in the air, as all the while Linus Gaynor lay on his bed listening, the strains of the singing just loud enough to creep up the wall of his house and across his room into his ears. No one could tell by looking at him what he was thinking.

Chapter Eight

In the weeks after he had confronted Linus Gaynor, Judge Olin Prescott was reminded of what an excellent lover he was. His exploits in bed began to interfere with his normal work as he frequently arrived for court sessions with the eyes dug deep into the back of his head and a barely concealed smile on his face. He had not had so much fun since his twenties, when he had been sure that as long as there was breath in his lungs and fire in his belly he would be a stupendous lover. It was difficult for him to say what had gone wrong with that forecast, but all of his notions of infinite sexual grandeur had frittered away in the first years of marriage, leading him to the depressing realisation that he no longer found his wife the slightest bit attractive. For twenty years they had both lived in that listless vessel, only coming together mechanically when they agreed it was time for children, otherwise keeping to their own sides of the bed where they watched the interminable movements of the large spiders which crossed their ceiling at night, and dreamed of ephemeral lovers.

During that twenty years, they both sought other interests to replace the love which their marriage had failed to sustain. In the case of the Judge's wife, she began to paint with a rapidity which quickly filled every room in the house to overflow with exhibits of dubious quality in the eyes of her husband. He could never see any beauty in what she painted and he dismissed those who did as being hopelessly inept in the art of criticism. He took upon himself the task of commenting on her works, condemning what she did with an almost perverted enthusiasm, but she took no notice of him, and her work continued to display the characteristics which he ridiculed so incessantly. The truth was that they were both correct: he in his criticism and she in ignoring it. For his part, the Judge began to collect lawnmowers in his shed. His weekends were devoted to roaming the capital's bric-à-brac shops in his herring-bone farmer's outfit, trying to pass himself off as a man of the countryside whose empire was so successful that he could find the time to rummage through the relics of his grandfather's times in search of these implements of ingenious simplicity. He never ceased to be enthralled at how the pressure of a human hand could set the mechanics in motion, the wheels falling silent again once the force was released. When he purchased a new machine, he would play with it for hours with greater interest than he had ever shown in his children, walking it along the path in front of his house, mesmerised by the revolving parts until he was almost in a trance, his eyes the size of pomegranates and his whole body tingling as if under the spell of a druid.

It is not inconceivable that Judge Olin Prescott and his wife would have remained on this course until the end of their lives had it not been for the Minister's decision to dispatch him to sort out the illicit situation in which Linus Gaynor had assumed the role of judge. After twenty years of living for nothing but bad water-colours and lawnmowers, the Judge and his wife seemed destined never to copulate again. It was impossible to tell if such a prospect upset either of them, for they never spoke about such things, but one thing did seem unquestionable, namely that the spirit of love was dead inside them and that nothing could revive it short of reincarnation.

It seemed to his wife that such a renewal had in fact begun, however, on the night the Judge returned home carrying a bouquet of yellow roses, the colour which he had at least remembered was her favourite, despite not having bought her flowers for twenty years. She had greeted him with growing incredulity when he had passed them to her and had taken the opportunity to kiss her lips and squeeze her shoulders with his small hands. Sitting in their vase on top of the ugly dresser which she had insisted on bringing from her late father's house, the flowers looked more like souvenirs than tokens of love. She had no idea why he had bought them for her, and so when she looked at them she thought only of the past, just as she did when she saw the photograph of her father which stood beside them and the overly ornate piece of furniture on which they rested.

It was not until they had gone to bed that the Judge's wife confirmed that there was indeed something different about her husband. To begin with he spent almost twenty minutes in the bathroom beautifying himself before he came to bed. This he had not done since the nights of their early marriage, and he now preened himself only in the mornings or before going to mass on Sundays, where the pious men carried out an unspoken joust to wear the most aromatic cologne – a rivalry which made certain areas of the church unspeakably odorous well into the middle of the week. When he emerged from the bathroom and crossed to the bed, the Judge stood momentarily by the small table on which he rested the book and the glass of water he always brought to bed with him. It seemed to his wife that he was thinking about something, his eyes looking down at the table for almost a minute before he notice-ably came to a decision, at which point he opened his bathrobe and revealed himself to be totally naked. Judge Olin Prescott's wife had to restrain herself from laughing, for the deterioration in his weaponry was more severe than she had imagined. But he seemed undeterred, climbing in beside her and taking her body in his arms in a workmanlike fashion as if he were lifting a bag of groceries.

Throughout the night, Judge Olin Prescott made love to his wife, who found herself willing to go along with him such was the persuasiveness of his touch. It was a routine which they were to repeat for the following three nights, an unparalleled display of lust culminat-ing in what he said to her before getting out of bed on the Friday morning. 'I love the bones of you,' he said, a sentiment which made her revise the impression of her husband she had collected over the years. His words were spoken so sincerely that she accepted she had been mistaken in thinking that he had grown to be a cold man, no longer capable of loving anything except the few hairs which offered a residue of hope for the top of his head. During the twenty years in which he had not spoken a single word of affection to her, she had abandoned all expectations of the heart, believing that if sweet nothings were ever again to be whispered into her ear they would not come from the mouth of her husband. Yet long after she had resigned herself to the death of their love-affair she was to hear him speak again the kind of words which had once been his stock in trade, and she believed him when he said them, because although she could accuse him of being many things through the years, a liar was not one of them, for she could not remember a single occasion when her husband had been untruthful.

But there was, of course, no truth in what Judge Olin Prescott said to his wife. He did not love her bones or any other part of her, but the upsurge of his libido had left him with a particular problem and he could think of no more quaint option but to satisfy this new friend by making love to his wife. Quite where his revived appetite had come from he was not sure, finding himself like a priest who discovers an abandoned baby on his doorstep, all eagerness to help but with little recent experience of what to do. But he accepted it with what he considered to be the right spirit, taking it as a gift rather than a burden, and went in search of the life he had once led. When he drove out of the city in the mornings he would look in his mirror and find on his mouth a broad smile which he had been unaware of. The orifice increasingly seemed to be acting of its own volition, smiling without permission as it gave away the renaissance in his bedroom. In the midst of all this smiling, Judge Olin Prescott gradually grew to care less about the condition of his hair, as if he no longer needed it to be in pristine order to feel attractive to women. But for all his smiling, Judge Olin Prescott was not a changed man inside. It was true that he was again practising the art of sex, but this was no indication that he had undergone any rebirth of compassion. Indeed this façade of merriment served to conceal the true Judge Olin Prescott, who had long since lost any sense of humanity, and who was now an even more dangerous man behind his new disguise of decency.

The extent of the lie that was Judge Olin Prescott's new face could best be seen from the severity of the sentences which he began to hand down for the pettiest of crimes. It was not just the size of the fines and the lengths of incarcerations which shocked the defendants, but that they were particularly unexpected at the end of cases which the Judge insisted be carried out in the friendliest of terms. He would set an example by referring to everyone by their Christian names. He would interrupt barristers in the course of their submissions and correct them for being too formal in their language, refusing to allow them to continue until they had given an undertaking to use names instead of titles. To those who had not heard of the Judge's new way of proceeding, his methods came as a complete surprise, and especially to those who knew they were guilty but who suspected that a man of such friendliness could not possibly deliver a severe sentence. It was these individuals who found themselves most confused by him. Passing sentence, he would speak to them as if he were a lifelong friend, his face bearing a wide smile of benign authority but his tongue delivering a punishment which belied his manner and bore no relation to the offence committed.

Returning at the end of each day, Judge Olin Prescott would spend a short time admiring the lights of the capital from a distance, a view which made him think of his wife and the night which lay ahead of him. In the weeks after they had started to love again, the Judge did not fail to return in the evening without a gift for her. When they had no more vases free to take flowers, he began to bring her expensive chocolates in golden boxes. These, she reminded him, made her fat, and so he brought her clothes instead. There was an air of chance about the garments he bought. He never asked her what size she took; instead he attempted to describe her to shop assistants and asked them to make a judgement as to what he should buy. Some of these purchases were more successful than others, but Judge Olin Prescott's wife began to fill her wardrobe with a range of haphazard outfits, some of which fitted her and some of which did not, and many she knew she would never wear in public.

It was in so many ways an artificial affair, sustained by her unwillingness to believe that he would suddenly contrive so great a lie after so many years of opportunity, and by his generosity in the place of affection. They were both prepared to continue in their new way in the certainty that this was their last chance to behave like lovers. For her part, the Judge's wife had persuaded herself that she could visibly follow the downward momentum of her flesh. 'If you look at me for long enough you can see me droop,' she confided in him. 'I'm slowly sinking into the floor.' That she was prepared to say such things to him was a perfect example of how far he had gone in deceiving her. The woman who just some weeks before had restrained her opinion of the weather in case she gave away some of her secrets was now dismantling the walls of her heart, allowing him an unhindered view of what lay inside. In all of his responses to her worries, he never gave away the truth that he did not care about her at any time of the day except the nights, when he had unfettered access to her body. And even then, even in the cold heat of false passion, he did not regard her as anything but the machine on which he could exercise his rediscovered penchant for sex. Such was the excellence of his subterfuge that she never knew she was lying down with a prince of charlatans.

When he was not deceiving his wife or handing down ridiculous sentences from his bench, Judge Olin Prescott liked to imagine what Linus Gaynor would be thinking at that time. Although he could not be sure of it, he had a growing suspicion that it was his encounter with this man which had reincarnated the instincts which had been lying dormant for so many bland years. The prospect of a truly magnificent fight was filling his loins with expectation, and at times he was tempted to believe that this encounter had been sent by God. But he would only think this for a short time before dismissing such an idea as religious fantasy. Every evening before going into his bathroom to make himself handsome he would look in his diary where he had marked with flamboyant calligraphy the date when he was due to return to the town where Linus Gaynor lay. To him this day replaced all others in importance in the calendar. It replaced Christmas day, which he had not enjoyed since the last of his children admitted to him that she no longer believed in Father Christmas. She had looked into his eyes and he into hers and had asked him to confirm or deny her logic. That was the last occasion on which Judge Olin Prescott could remember being touched by an emotion. It was the end of his fatherhood. He had never lied to his children except on those occasions where it was expected of a father to lie in the cause of innocence. On this occasion he took his young daughter in his arms and hugged her for the last time as a believer in Santa Claus before telling her that she was right in her conclusion. Since that year he had never again enjoyed the twenty-fifth of December. Many other days had also been replaced by the extravagantly illuminated day in his diary: his own birthday, which he had for many years tried to forget existed; the anniversary of his marriage, which was always marked by an awkward silence of contrition; even the annual celebration of his elevation to the bench no longer held any great significance for him, except that it marked the day on which he was given the instruments with which to dismantle the court of Linus Gaynor.

Now this day which had been emblazoned in his diary became the focal point of his future. He counted down the days to it as if waiting for his summer holidays. With each passing day he turned the pages of his diary with an elaborate sweep of his arm, like a preacher turning the page of the liturgy. He even began to suffer nightmares over it, waking in the early hours in a sweat and shouting to himself having dreamt that the Minister had instructed him to abandon the case of Linus Gaynor. Such an instruction would have been a catastrophe for him, and his wife found him sitting up in bed pleading with an invisible politician to allow him to continue his crusade for justice. So great was the importance of this cause to him that he sold his collection of lawnmowers to an ironmonger on the condition that the collection be broken up, for he could no longer give it the attention its artistry demanded and he knew that there was no other man alive could tend it with equal adoration. 'Break it up,' he said to the ironmonger. 'Send them to the four corners of the country, for I alone could make them unique.'

On the Saturday morning before he returned to Poule, Judge Olin Prescott rose from his bed earlier than even he was used to doing. It was so early that the blackbirds were not yet about, so, to avenge the annoyance they had so often caused him, he yelled at the trees where they nested, sending them flurrying in the air before their usual time. He went into his bathroom and greased his hair for what he was sure would be the last time, before getting into his car and driving to the Inns of Court where he had booked a very early appointment with the judges' barber. Saturday mornings were always set aside for the judges. Because they were older than most of the other customers, they generally had less hair and so a visit to the barbers seemed a more unnecessary journey than for most. But the judges would convene on a Saturday morning like a therapy group of substance abusers, sitting along the wall with their row of identical heads – each one bald with a flowing strand laid across the top in the manner of an ill-secured and tasteless carpet. For years Judge Olin Prescott had been a member of this ensemble, and his cultivated strands had been treated with meticulous respect by the barber for fear of leaving some part of the crown overexposed, which would bring down on him a torrent of abuse culminating in the derision of his working-class origins. The reason for Judge Olin Prescott's unusually early appointment was that he had come to have his cranial accessory amputated. He entered the shop with great purpose for the time of day and instructed the barber to cut it off. 'Off with it,' he insisted. 'Off with the whole shootin' gallery of it.' The barber asked again if the Judge was sure, and in truth he would have been happier to have had his instructions in writing, but Judge Olin Prescott assured him that he had heard correctly. 'Come on, for God's sake,' said the Judge. 'Cut it off before anyone arrives.'

Judge Olin Prescott left the barber shop by the back door in case he met any of his colleagues arriving to have their follicles pampered. It was not that he was ashamed of what he had just done or that he was having second thoughts about his rashness. He simply did not think that he could stand the questions they would ask him, insinuating deep in the syntax of their enquiries that he was a traitor for doing such a thing and that now they might all have to follow suit to avoid accusations of being unable to accept the awful stigmata of ageing. He knew that he would no longer be popular with them. This did not worry him, for he had only ever maintained civility in their company to make his occupation bearable. But he knew that from then on he would be regarded with disdain for his exposing the truth about their heads. None of this worried Judge Olin Prescott as he drove through the awakening city in the beautiful privacy of the early morning. Again he could not help but admire the face of his city. At such a time of the day the light was unforgiving as it picked out every crack. But he still saw the place as marvellous – perhaps the one thing in the world which had remained immune to the eroding cynicism of his advancing years.

On the Sunday morning he was again up early, but this time he did not spend his usual period interned in the bathroom. In fact when they walked to the church his wife noticed the difference through the absence of the choking smell of extravagant aftershave. As they took their seat where they always sat, his nose was assaulted for the first time by the overpowering scent of the other men. Like an abstainer among hobos, he alone could smell the cologne from their bodies, and he thought that he would vomit as he journeyed through the yawning steppes of another endless sermon.

On the night before he returned to Poule, the Judge's wife lay on their bed waiting for him, her body unclothed and shining from the expensive oils he had bought her. She lay for an hour until her patience was almost at an end, and when she thought it was time to shout to him to come to bed he arrived fully clothed and exuding all the frigidity which had marked the past twenty years of their marriage. In his eyes she saw his contempt for her, and in an instant it was clear to her that they had had intercourse for the last time. 'Stop making such a fool of yourself,' he said to her – 'you have nothing that I want.' She did not know whether to laugh or cry, but most of all she wanted to kill him for the completeness of his deceit. She felt totally violated, as pierced as if he had driven a sabre through her gut, and without interruption she never again considered herself as anything but a married harlot.

By the morning Judge Olin Prescott had forgotten how wicked his eyes had been the previous night. He was woken by the noise of the hundred blackbirds who plagued his trees and shat everywhere they could find. In the twenty-five years he had lived in that house, the ammonia in the birds' shit had defaced many of the statuettes his wife had installed about the gardens. The birds were a constant source of annoyance to the Judge, who had promised himself some years before that the day would come when he would take a rifle to the birds and an axe to the trees, in the belief that such a combination of remedies would rid him once and for all of the scourge of heavenly shit. But he paid no attention to that problem this morning. In fact he did not even notice the splashes on the windscreen of his car, which he had washed and polished the previous day as he felt a man of his importance should have a car which looked the part. As he drove out of the city, he took one last look at it and counted himself lucky to have such a place to return to when the rigours of crime became difficult to bear. In the countryside he was less at ease, and it was only then that he noticed the shit on his window, which sent him into a torrent of abuse after which he stopped and removed the stain with a tuft of dandelion leaves.

Even from a distance of half a mile, Judge Olin Prescott could feel the gaze of a hundred pairs of eyes watching out for him, and he could feel the straining of ears taking in every sound of the morning in search of the noise of his car. When he reached the house where Linus Gaynor lay he was not surprised to see a group of lunatics standing in a huddle, warming themselves with the heat of each other's body against the chill of a winter day. The Judge did not slow down as he passed the house, but from the corner of his eye he could see the curtain of an upstairs window being held back by a hand. He drove on until he reached the American Hotel, where he parked his car and began his walk to the police station. There were a few people in the streets, and of these he most noticed Meabh Slevin running in the direction of her house, her eyes looking in a different direction – this time right at the Judge. But yet again she failed to fulfil his wish by colliding with anything. 'That woman has the instincts of a bat,' he thought to himself, and continued his short walk for the reunion with Police Sergeant Donald Kilgallon, who this time had planned to pander to officialdom by the immaculate condition of his office.

'Good morning, Sir,' said the Judge walking through the Sergeant's door. 'This is all very impressive.' Police Sergeant Donald Kilgallon was taken aback by the instant success of his pristine surroundings, and quickly sought to capitalise on his popularity by informing the Judge that he had a busy morning ahead of him in the Farmers' Hall. 'Excellent,' said Judge Olin Prescott without believing a word. 'Let's make a start then.'

It did not take long for Judge Olin Prescott to assure himself that he had been correct in assuming that he would hear nothing but fictitious cases on his return to the town. In his first case, Victor O'Shaughnessy was demanding compensation from Oliver Bermingham,

175

brother of Milo, for the sale of an unworthy car which refused to start after the first week. Right from the moment Victor O'Shaughnessy opened his mouth, Judge Olin Prescott marked him as a bad actor. Through all of his deposition he only twice looked the Judge in the eyes. This was his most critical imperson-ating flaw, for in all his years' experience, the Judge had come to recognise the truth of a plaintiff's case by the regularity of his eye contact. In the past Judge Olin Prescott had found himself having to look away from plaintiffs, such was the power of their gaze, but Victor O'Shaughnessy pursued his claim with all the verve of an overfed dog, his eyes looking everywhere but at the man he was trying to convince, and it was only for the humour of it that the Judge allowed him to speak for ten minutes before stopping him and dismissing the case.

It was to be no different with his next case, in which Eoin Danagher was seeking slander damages against Una Cash for calling him a drunken buffoon in front of all the customers in her public bar. Like Victor O'Shaughnessy, Eoin Danagher could not bring him-self to look at Judge Olin Prescott's eyes, and through his reticence he gave away the badly concealed truth that the alleged incident had never taken place except in the realms of make-believe. Not only did he not look at Judge Olin Prescott, but his hands began to tremble in unison with his voice, a symptom which the Judge was certain had nothing to do with the emotion of the moment but was merely the rapid peeling away of a façade to reveal the lie beneath. 'I think I'd better stop you now,' said Judge Olin Prescott, 'because you are a liar for sure. I doubt this woman ever called you a drunken buffoon, but if she did I would have to find for her as it is entirely true.'

As the morning began to drag, Judge Olin Prescott found his patience becoming thinner and thinner. With each succeeding trial he was less able to see the joke in the spectacle of bad acting, and he could feel his insides beginning to heat up like a volcano as the scale of the lying became clear. Sergeant Donald Kilgallon had not been untruthful when he said that he would have a busy morning, for with every case he threw out another appeared at the door in the guise of two incompetent liars. But he had agreed with himself beforehand that he would sit through all that was brought before him until midday, in the remote hope that from among the fiction a real case might emerge to light up his morning. But remaining until midday was all he would tolerate. This was the last chance he was prepared to give them, and if by then no one of integrity had come before him, he would order the doors of the hall to be closed and declare an end to the rigged proceedings.

It seemed to the Judge that it took a month for the clock to move on by two hours. For a time he even wished that he had his strands of hair again so he would have something to occupy him as he sat through the hideous concoction of fairy tales which came to torment him. Not in one of them did he detect the slightest suspicion of truth, nor did he feel able to admit to himself that the perpetrators of this drivel were convincing in any way. Few of them lasted for more than ten minutes before he banged his gavel on the table and ordered them to be quiet and leave, and when the clock at last made its way around to midday he declared the court finished for the day with a feeling of enormous relief, and went to get some fresh air.

Judge Olin Prescott had not been able to tell from his seat in the Farmers' Hall that it had started to rain. It was not a heavy rain but the fine drizzle that his grandmother had warned him was the most dangerous as it could penetrate every kind of clothing and reach your bones, where only years after a soaking would its harvest of rheumatism emerge like a vampire. The ground was very wet so he guessed it had been raining for quite some time, the steady monotonous fall matching everything he had heard indoors that morning. But in a way he welcomed it. He walked without a coat or an umbrella and with total disregard for the premonitions of his grandmother, sensing that the water was cooling the temper which had been brewing in his stomach all morning. He never liked it when he was completely angry, for he believed it affected him in the way that alcohol affected some of his colleagues, blurring their effectiveness in a way that was visible to all except the drinker. 'A bad temper is like an unfaithful lover,' he once warned an unruly barrister: 'in the end it will be the ruin of you.'

The Judge continued to walk in the dreary rain for over twenty minutes, during which time his clothes became quite wet and his temper formed into the sharpened implement of justice which he knew would be necessary to instigate the procedure which he had suspected would be required from the first moment he ever walked into the town. He put direction into his previously random meandering and walked to the police station, where he found Donald Kilgallon and informed him that they were going to the house of Linus Gaynor to place him under arrest for impersonating a judge.

The Police Sergeant was not surprised that Judge Olin Prescott had not believed any of the cases which had come before him that morning, for he had himself watched the first three litigations and had come to an early conclusion that the acting was so bad it was all a lost cause. He had spent the rest of the morning in his office wondering whether or not he should write a letter of resignation, for he was sure the Judge would have him divested of his stripes at best, and at worst would have him thrown from the force as an accessory in deception. But Judge Olin Prescott made no mention of his involvement in the abysmal dramatics that had been enacted that morning. Instead he summoned the Police Sergeant from his office like he would have done a dog, calling him with quick movements of his forefinger and pointing to the ground behind his heels to indicate the distance which the Police Sergeant was to keep from him.

As they marched in tandem down the street in the direction of Poule, the purpose in the Judge's steps told all of those who saw him that this was a matter of gravity. As they walked, Judge Olin Prescott noticed that the rain was growing heavier. He was by now beginning to feel the water against his skin, but he had no concern that in future years it might cripple him with pain, for now he had only one thing on his mind and that was the destruction of the court of Linus Gaynor.

It was Meabh Slevin who followed them most closely as they walked, her stunted legs requiring her to run in order to keep pace. She too had noticed how much heavier the rain had become, and it was to her mind first came the notion that this was water from the ducts of heaven, the tears of God falling on a dark day just as it had been on Good Friday at the moment Christ perished. This was a parable she was to repeat time and again in her accounts of that day, and in her bloated memory the rain was to become a torrent when in fact it was no more than a healthy shower, though enough to soak the Judge and his escort, who nevertheless ignored it as if it was a pestilent beggar who did not understand the importance of their journey.

It would be entirely correct to say that it was no surprise to Gretchen Gaynor to open her front door and find Judge Olin Prescott standing in a posture which exuded malice from every pore of his small face, behind him the dishevelled figure of Police Sergeant Donald Kilgallon, who would have swapped his position for a place in hell. She, like everyone else, had been aware since quite soon after the fake proceedings of the morning had begun that the elaborate scheme of deception had collapsed pitifully through the inexperience of the actors – a facet of its perpetration whose importance they had underestimated in the avalanche of ideas submitted once the Judge's perilous intentions were made obvious. So, not only was Gretchen Gaynor not surprised by her visitors, but she had in fact been expecting them to call and in such an anticipation she had prepared an unwelcoming visage which left the Judge in no doubt that he was entering hostile territory.

In the room where Linus Gaynor lay, Judge Olin Prescott announced to him that he was to be placed under arrest for judicial impersonation, and with that he stepped aside to allow the Police Sergeant to formally confirm the fact. Standing at the end of Linus Gaynor's bed, Donald Kilgallon mumbled his words of caution and with every syllable he grunted his stuttering voice pleaded for forgiveness for what he was being ordered to do. In addition to placing Linus Gaynor under arrest, Judge Olin Prescott informed him that he was not to leave the jurisdiction. 'I will spare you the ordeal of a police cell,' said the Judge, feigning magnanimity, 'but from now on, you and anyone who comes to visit you are criminals. Even those you have the effrontery to declare innocent will be guilty. Anyone who comes near you for advice will be contaminated by your guilt. You had better watch yourself, you know. You had better watch everything you blink your eyes about, for I will want to know if you have even given an opinion on the weather. In short, you would be better keeping everything to yourself. Not a hint of what you think is anyone's business but yours from now on, and I promise you that if you try to disobey me again I will have you locked away where you cannot even see whether the sun is shining.'

Gretchen Gaynor managed to contain her ferocious anger while in her husband's presence, for she knew he would not want her to embroil herself in a direct confrontation with the Judge. But by the time she had escorted the Judge to the bottom of her stairs she could remain silent no longer. Like opening a saloon door, she burst into a stream of abuse. 'You're a disgrace and a fool,' she roared at him. 'If you think you'll stop Linus Gaynor from being the man he is you're mistaken. He has more strength in his eyelids than you have in your back. You're a coward beyond shame, a coward without eyes, for all you have to do is look around you and see the order he has brought. There's more happiness here than you can ever claim credit for creating. Not in all your years of inherited authority can you have achieved the respect which Linus Gaynor has earned for himself from the confines of his bed. You'll regret having come here today. Linus Gaynor was not spared by God to submit to the whims of an insect like you.' Blown by the gales of her temper, Judge Olin Prescott reached the gate of Gretchen Gaynor's garden quicker than he had imagined, Police Sergeant Donald Kilgallon behind him already considering his resignation letter for the second time in an hour.

They returned to the police station as they had come: Judge Olin Prescott in front and at his heels the figure of Police Sergeant Donald Kilgallon, whose head had slipped forward and down so that his chin now rested on his sternum. 'Do you know that I am almost disappointed by what I have just seen, Sergeant?' said the Judge without bothering to look back at the man he was speaking to. 'It is not at all the cabal of monsters I had expected. There was only that woman – something of a witch to be sure, but I have been called worse by worse. Mark my words, Sergeant, there is only one thing more forlorn than a man who believes he can change the world and that is the woman who believes him when he says it.'

They continued to walk in the steady rain without either of them looking to the side. 'The Black Death, Sergeant,' said the Judge: 'during its worst ravages people used to pile the corpses high and set them alight. Then as the fire burned they would dance around it. That is all that is happening here, you know. They are all just dancing around the pyre. It's a ritual of denial. You take your worst fear and dance with it, like it's your suitor.'

'It sounds like a wake to me, Sir,' replied the Police Sergeant.

'No, it is not like a wake, Sergeant,' said the Judge quickly. 'It is not death they are trying to spite: it is decay, disorder, disharmony, and if I were not a judge I would find that commendable. But I am a judge and you are a policeman, and if there is to be harmony here then we are to be its guardians.'

'Even if we have to destroy to create it?' said the Police Sergeant.

'It is not creation we are interested in, Sergeant: it is containment. We are containers. If you wanted to be a creator you should have become a poet.'

When her eyes were no longer insulted by the sight of Judge Olin Prescott, Gretchen Gaynor became suddenly aware of the depth of the cold carried by the wind which blew from the direction the two men had gone. She did not go back to see her husband. He would have heard the abuse she levied on the Judge and she knew he would not have approved, for he always wished her to remain serene in the face of such adversities. Instead she took her red coat with the fake fur collar and set off in search of bearers who would swear on their fathers' graves that they would come in an instant to carry Linus Gaynor to safety if ever there was word received that Judge Olin Prescott wished to take him to prison. This was her most desperate moment. It seemed that all the events which had occurred in recent years were coming to a head in the shape of an attempt to deny Linus Gaynor the ability to practise the gifts she believed God had sent to him with the same hand which had rendered his limbs lifeless and his mouth a silent relic.

She did not have to go far before her path was blocked by neighbours who had been watching from their established vantage points. From behind the emerging hyacinths which she grew as Christmas presents, Banba Buckley had seen the two men march away in tandem as they had come, the Judge with an air of vindictiveness and the Police Sergeant muttering words of condolence to himself. Banba Buckley came out into the street and embraced Gretchen Gaynor with both arms until she sensed her asthma reasserting itself. They were joined by Eamonn Austin Phillip Peadar Gaynor, who had contemplated throwing missiles at the Judge and his escort from the secrecy of the fuchsia bush where he had camouflaged himself with a brownish beret and a pocket full of limestone. 'They were too far away from me,' he said as an apology, 'but next time I will be closer.'

The more that came out on to the street to speak with Gretchen Gaynor, the more there were who volunteered to carry her husband away in the event of danger. They were, without exception, shocked by the news that Linus Gaynor was under arrest, as shocked as they were by Judge Olin Prescott's callousness in disrupting their peace in such a way. It was no way to treat a man in Linus Gaynor's condition, they agreed, to threaten him with incarceration despite the imprisonment which he had been suffering for so many years and which they all knew would not release him until the day they carried him to join the other men in the cemetery. 'It is abominable,' shouted Kevin Daly. 'I have rarely heard such a thing as this. It shames us all as people.'

When she returned to the room where Linus Gaynor lay, Gretchen sat on the bed beside him and took him in her arms as she often did in the early evenings when they could watch the winter sun go down in half an hour. She told him that she wanted him to answer one question for her. If he did so truthfully then there would never be a time when she would ask him to justify anything again. 'Tell me you believe that what you are doing is right,' she said, and watching his eyelids with her neck bent down so it hurt her, she saw him blink once. 'Tell me again you are sure,' she said, and he blinked once again.

When the sun was completely gone she got up from the bed and went to her kitchen where she took down the tin box which had once been presented to her on her birthday, filled with sugar biscuits, and which she now used to store ink and paper. She sat by the gaslight near the fire and began to write a letter to Darius Gaynor, who had not come to see his father since the day he had refused for the third time to agree to Darius's marriage to Roberta Staunton. In her letter Gretchen Gaynor told her eldest son that his father was under arrest and in mortal danger of being imprisoned. She told him of how much she was afraid of his being suffocated behind layers of gates through which he would not emerge alive.

Chapter Nine

On the morning he received the letter from his mother, Darius Gaynor had been trying to convince himself and Roberta Staunton that they were fortunate people. He was able to point to their home. This had been rented at short notice and so at an exorbitant price from a Montenegrin refugee who had jumped ship in 1918 without even owning the clothes on his back, but was eventually able to proclaim himself a millionaire without anyone seeing in his lifestyle any reason to doubt his boasts. Despite the size of the rent, which Darius described as racketeering, they were both more in love than they had imagined possible. Within the walls of their affection they had insulated themselves against the gloomy chill of a world going mad. It was a happiness which was almost complete, lacking only an approving blink from Linus Gaynor, who continued to withhold his consent on grounds which Darius suspected involved supremacy.

When the postman Laurence O'Leary walked up their path to the front door, Darius Gaynor was looking out the front window at a neighbour collecting the shit from the milk-float horse which made his roses blossom like fireworks. From the face of his postman, Darius could sense that the news was confusing, for thirty years as a messenger had taught Laurence O'Leary to recognise the tone of a letter from the condition of the envelope and the handwriting on the front. When he handed the letter to Darius, the postman told him that he was sure he was unsure whether the news was good or bad, the envelope containing mixed tidings which it was for the reader to judge.

When he had finished reading the letter from his mother, Darius Gaynor could not have imagined Laurence O'Leary's diagnosis to have been more accurate. He felt his heart shudder at the spectre of the man he had grown to dislike being deprived of the one thing which kept him alive, and not for the first time since his father had refused to sanction his marriage did Darius Gaynor find himself prepared to look again at his father's reasons in a desperate search for an altruistic excuse. But try as he did he could find none, yet he confirmed to Roberta Staunton that he would return to Poule to see for himself the mounting danger in which his father had placed himself.

When Darius Gaynor did return to Poule, he chose to do so on a Wednesday morning. The town was quieter then, as many of the people had gone to market ten miles away to sell their animals to purchase furniture and radios. The night before he went he spent two hours cleaning his truck, which had not felt the touch of soapy water for some time. Inside the cab he polished the seats again just as his father used to. He cleaned the truck with considerable caution for nothing about the vehicle gave him much optimism that it would survive another year of pounding on the desperate country roads. But he cleaned it anyway, as a mark of respect and in the hope that by putting a decent shine on it he would also find it in himself to speak to his father with a civility which would be returned by common sense and a willingness to put an end to the turmoil which threatened to ruin a large part of both of their lives. From his wardrobe which nourished a thousand woodworm he took his brown suit with the grey pinstripe. Although it still fitted him, he could not believe as he looked at himself in the half mirror hanging on the bedroom door that he had once admired the piece of cloth so much that he had parted with honest money for it. It was not that fashion had changed, just that he had grown to hate the suit, for he only ever seemed to wear it on occasions of trouble. But he had nothing to put on in its place, so he brushed it down until it was as clean as he could make it and told Roberta Staunton that he did not know how long he would be gone.

As he drove out of the capital where they had set up their temporary home, Darius Gaynor unknowingly took the same road that Judge Olin Prescott had now travelled on several occasions. Unlike the Judge, Darius did not look back at the city, which he never liked to remain in for more than a few hours at a time, the noise of the traffic and the smell of dirty smoke being too intense for him to see any beauty in the place. It was only when he was back in the countryside that he felt secure again, away from the dangerous streets with their blackguards and lousy dogs. There a soul could at least be alone if he so wished, and even the decay of winter filled him with a sense of the replenishment of time. This was a wonderment which was exaggerated by his exile, and as he drove through the small villages with their haphazard architecture and passed the cold fields where the sheep and cattle ate incessantly, he was moved as rarely before by the surroundings of his birth, the kinds of places in which he had lingered in the flashing revelry of his youth.

When he reached Poule he could see no one about, for which he was grateful because he did not think he could sustain any conversation which would inevitably turn to the reasons for his absence. He knocked on the door, for he had returned his key in protest when he left, and when Gretchen Gaynor opened it she grabbed him much as she must have done in the first moments of his life when he became her first child. 'I never doubted for a minute that you would come,' she said, 'but I prayed that it would be this quickly.' They stood for several minutes by the door, embracing without intention to part, until the sight of Meabh Slevin's intrusive eyes looking at them as she ran with a demi-john in her arms made Gretchen shut the door and lead her son to the kitchen, where she poured him a bowl of steaming chicken soup.

It was while he was drinking his mother's most delicious concoction that the two of them began a conversation the likes of which they had never had before. They had grown to know each other well, or so they thought, but it was only in that moment which they were both to remember for the rest of their lives that they spoke with an honesty which often seemed to hurt as they peeled away the shells of their hearts and divulged their most terrible fears. Gretchen Gaynor admitted that her nights had become hosts to dreams in which her husband was taken from her to a place of stupefying remoteness. She could see him there in her imagination, but there was no way she could go and sit with him. These dreams she knew were the nocturnal shadows of the real-life threat of his imprisonment. 'He will die if they take him,' she said to Darius, 'yet he will die if he stops what he's doing.'

In response to his mother's fears, which seemed to have accelerated her ageing, Darius Gaynor told her that he believed his father had forbidden his marriage because he feared that he, Darius, would usurp the position as the figure of most responsibility. 'I have no wish to do such a thing,' said Darius – 'all I want is for us to live in the way I think God meant us to do.'

Gretchen Gaynor told her son that his father had no grudge against Roberta Staunton or against him. 'You are right, but he is afraid of dying,' she said, 'and the only reason he has left to live is that he controls this family. If you take that away from him then he has nothing.'

When they had finished speaking, Darius left his mother in the kitchen and went up the stairs to his father's bedroom, closing the door behind him with the delicate touch he always used when entering in case Linus Gaynor was sleeping. Gretchen listened for a moment, following her son's footsteps across the bedroom floor until she heard the faint sound of his voice speaking to his father. Then she began to clear away the dirty dishes from the table, praying silently to herself that her son's visit would begin the mending which she so dearly wanted.

By the time she had finished washing the dishes Darius Gaynor had still not emerged from his father's room. She took this to be a promising sign, as on the previous two occasions when he had come in search of approval he had stormed out quickly. This time Gretchen Gaynor could sense that things were different. She could not be sure if this had been caused by the intervention of the Judge or whether her husband had considered his situation long enough to finally see that his son had no designs on his position as head of the family. Whatever the reason, over an hour passed during which she could still hear the calm voice of her son speaking to his father in a way he had not done for too long. Frustrated by not knowing what was going on, she considered sneaking to the top of the stairs and listening, but this would have been to break her solemn pledge made years before and which to that day had remained intact. This of all occasions, she told herself, would not be the time to go against her own promises – not when the matter involved her own son. So she took her red coat with the fake white fur collar and went out into the street in search of someone to talk to.

She first saw Ursula Bancroft, who had come out to buy flour as she had done every morning since she read of the outbreak of the Spanish Civil War. This event, she was convinced, was the prelude to the destruction of civilisation. 'God will bless Generalissimo Franco,' she had insisted then, 'at the very least he will sit with the vanquished in heaven.' In the three years since it had happened, she had fastidiously hoarded as much flour as she could afford, a quantity which she now reckoned to be sufficient for her to survive for one year without the need to venture outside her door where her head was likely to become the target for an anarchist's bullet. Ursula Bancroft barely stopped to acknowledge the greetings of Gretchen Gaynor before concentrating her mind again on the task of safely transporting her precious cargo to the sanctuary of her kitchen. Donie Campbell was about too, his big nose obvious from a distance as he swept and reswept the pavement outside his fishing-tackle shop, a habit which alleviated the boredom of the lack of customers at that time of year.

Gretchen Gaynor walked on until she stood outside the Catholic church. With its two modest towers, one of which held the bell that frightened the children when it roared out its call to mass in the mornings, it looked like a miniature cathedral. Like many of its age, the church had been built with its back to the street, a contrast to its Protestant rival which stood at the fork in the road, its long gravel path leading from the gate to the doors with a line of blue Atlas cedars on either side. It was in the church with its back to the street that she had had her children baptised, and with nothing else to accompany her but time, she went in and sat near the statue of the Blessed Oliver Plunkett, who had been martyred in 1681. There she remained for what she guessed must have been half an hour. She could only estimate this as she refused to carry a timepiece in case it enslaved her as one had done her father – a man who was so possessed by time that he would only pee every seventh half hour, even if his bladder threatened to explode inside him. Gretchen Gaynor had spared herself the torture of such an outlook and looked with pity on those who punished themselves with time. It often meant that she was late for appointments, but she dismissed this by claiming a woman's privilege and boasting that she did not believe that time was anything but a device invented to sell clocks.

When she returned to the street the weather had again turned wet and miserably cold. It was only on occasions like these that the fake extravagance of her coat gave itself away, the wind cutting through the material like a hundred freezing blades, scraping at her skin until her jaw vibrated up and down so much that she had to hold it shut with her hand. In the kitchen at Poule she found Darius Gaynor pouring himself some more soup, as the temperature in his father's room had dipped while he was there. He was full of idle talk to begin with, commenting on things which had been in the house for all of his childhood and never before

seemed worthy of his conversation. From his condition, Gretchen Gaynor sensed that her son was grap-
pling with serious news, for he was showing no sign of
speaking to her of his time with Linus Gaynor. 'Will
you tell me what happened, for God's sake?' she said to
him.

'He has relented,' said Darius. 'He has given his
consent to our marriage. Everything is settled.'

Although Darius Gaynor assured his mother that his
father's decision had not demanded anything in
return, she felt that if that was the case then her son
should have accepted the news with greater merriment
than he was showing. Upset by his calm, she asked him
again if his father had lain down conditions for his
decision, but Darius replied again that he had not.
When she questioned him about the serenity which he
was displaying, he told her that it was simply his shock
at the reversal of Linus Gaynor's mind and that in time
he would come to celebrate this in full. With that he
told his mother that it was time for him to leave as he
had to go in search of Father Raymond Curtis to ask
him to officiate at the wedding.

On his way to the presbytery where he hoped to find
the enormous priest, Darius Gaynor passed a group of
lunatics who were standing by the gable wall of the
house, completely ignoring the rain and the wind as
they mumbled to themselves in words he could not
understand. The street of the town was otherwise still
deserted, as it would remain well into the afternoon,
when the traders would return either celebrating a
prosperous day in which case they would be heard
from a distance, or else skulking into their homes in
despair to hide themselves until the wounds of com-
merce had been healed. It was not a long journey to the
presbytery and Darius did not think it worthwhile

starting up his engine, as the battery had for weeks been showing the unmistakable signs of exhaustion. As he approached the building, he noticed for the first time the dilapidated condition of the garden and the façade. This had never been the case before, as previous occupants had always considered it a responsibility to present an image of order, if only limited to the outside of the building, but Darius Gaynor was in no doubt that the tradition had been broken during the tenure of Father Raymond Curtis.

Darius Gaynor did not know that the reason for the dishevelled appearance of the building was that no one found it possible any longer to work for the priest, who had deteriorated into a state of utter depression as he watched the collapse of rationalism around him. In the previous two months he had hired two new housekeepers, but both of them had resigned within a week, complaining of Father Raymond Curtis's hopeless expectations of them given his habit of littering the rooms which they had just cleaned. In addition to such antisocial behaviour, he had also insisted on drinking whiskey from the kitchen mugs, which he would then smash against the skullery wall as if he was a Cossack. There had been times when the housekeepers believed he had taken deliberate aim at them before hurling the mugs, the women having to duck quickly to avoid the full force of the utensils on the chin. Such working conditions were impossible, they had protested to him, yet he showed no signs of remorse for his behaviour and accepted their resignations by laughing into their faces.

The experience of Aoife Quill had been little better. For over eleven years she had tended the garden of the presbytery, her hefty bottom being a regular sight during the summers, stuck up in the air like a suspended

Friesian as she tended the plants with all the skills of an aged midwife. But even Aoife Quill, who had been able to laugh off years of smutty remarks or whistles with sexual intonations when men laid their eyes on her expansive posterior, even she could not remain in the employment of Father Raymond Curtis, who had come to speak to her in words bearing abuse and ridicule. In the final moment of her degradation by his innuendo, she had almost lain waste the garden which had been the beneficiary of her blessed hands through the years, the catastrophe being averted only by a sudden surge of pity to her head. In the absence of the housekeepers, the windows bore the spotted stains of rainfall, and in the garden the ground proffered no signs of Miss Aoife Quill's ordained fertility.

When Darius Gaynor knocked on the door of the presbytery, the sound of the call reverberated through the building like the draught of a moving ghost, and he listened for some moments before he heard the sound of Father Raymond Curtis coming to the door, one footstep indistinguishable from the next, his whole body shuffling forward as if on wheels. Darius Gaynor had not been sure what to expect on the other side of the door, but when it had been pulled open there stood the great priest in his black trousers and jersey, his chin bearing the scars of a cold shave and his eyes looking out with a watery glare.

'Come in, Darius,' said the priest standing aside, his temper abated by the absence of recent alcohol, and his mind temporarily distracted from the sermon he was writing on the virtues of wine. It had been some time since anyone had come to see him at the presbytery, for no one considered it a good idea to meet him there, so his warm welcome for Darius Gaynor was the product as much of surprise as it was of the affinity he felt for

195

the young man as a fellow sufferer at the hands of Linus Gaynor. 'I would offer you a whiskey,' he said, 'only if I start now I will not finish until I am too drunk to find my bed.' Darius Gaynor accepted his apology and assured him that he did not want a drink, then he went on to tell the priest why he had come to see him.

'I've come about my wedding,' said Darius.

'But you're not having one,' replied Father Raymond Curtis quickly, holding his head in his right hand and running his fingers through his hair. 'You're not allowed to have a wedding, I should say,' continued the priest raising his voice, 'because an order has been given. A silent order – oh, a very silent order – but I have never heard such a booming silence in my life. It seems that every time your father closes his eyelids in a negative gesture, they slam shut like the gates of Derry. And perhaps we will still be celebrating their closing in another 250 years' time. For it appears that we are to be the fodder of history, Darius. You and I are to be guillotined by your father's eyelids, garrotted against his bedpost. But there is no reason for us to fear. Why should we complain when our sacrifices are the cobblestones for such sacred feet? If we are to be walked upon, then we might as well be walked upon by a deity. So you must accept it, Darius, and hope that historians at least have the decency to mention your obedience, for it is unlikely they will care to mention your pain.'

But Darius interrupted him before he could go any further. 'No, you don't understand,' he said. 'I am to get married. My father has given his consent. He's changed his mind. That's why I've come.'

On hearing Darius's story, Father Raymond Curtis felt that he had lost a friend. He felt that the two of them were no longer united in their purgatory and, inasmuch as this upset him, he did not even think to congratulate the young man on his news. Instead he considered telling Darius that he would not consent to his request on the grounds that his father was a religious impostor who distracted the minds of the people with pretensions of magic. But he contained himself long enough to say that he would consider the matter, telling Darius that he first wished to speak to his father about it.

Father Raymond Curtis led Darius Gaynor to the door, where he himself saw for the first time with any clarity the condition in which his garden lay. It embarrassed him so much that he maintained a trivial conversation with his visitor until they reached the gate. By doing so he hoped that Darius would not have time to cast an eye over the wilderness and might be inclined to believe that rumours of the priest's fading integrity were to be regarded as nothing more than malice.

When he returned to the privacy of his house, Father Raymond Curtis was faced with what he would later acknowledge to be the most awful moment of his life. The full extent of his degradation became clear to him, and in a moment of error he looked at himself in the cracked mirror which hung on the bathroom door. What he saw made his stomach turn as it had never done before, not even when he confronted the most detested outcasts of humanity in the capital's prison where he alone would administer sacraments to the murderous paedophiles. 'Oh my God,' he whispered to himself, 'I look like a poet.' He filled his bath to almost overflowing and immersed himself in the lukewarm water without even realising the modest temperature. There he remained for an hour, wallowing like a hog, fully submerged except for his knees, which were forced out of the water by the length of his legs, and for those parts of his body necessary for breathing. No one was to see him, but if they did they might have thought

197

the presbytery had been visited by a leviathan which stayed motionless for all that time while its brain pondered the extent to which it had allowed things to deteriorate.

When he was finished, Father Raymond Curtis rose up out of the dirty mire and after drying himself with a damp towel he strode naked to his bedroom, where he noticed the smell of bad socks and opened the window for the first time in a month. He dressed himself that day full of renewed hope. Darius Gaynor's news seemed to hold out the possibility that Linus Gaynor had undergone a change of heart since he had dismissed Father Raymond Curtis's pleas for sanity with the mesmerising blow of his silence. Putting on a pair of darned socks, Father Raymond Curtis noticed himself singing *Bridín Ban Mo Stór*, a ditty which he had always sung when in good spirits. Now it had come to him without a summons – an indication, he concluded, that the dormant bones of hope were stirring again inside him. He dressed himself as he had done in the days before his trouble, donning each garment with the meticulous care appropriate to a messenger of God, until he stood handsome and clean amid the rubble of his unfortunate recent past which he vowed to clear away once he had been to visit Linus Gaynor.

In the street outside, Meabh Slevin was so surprised at what she saw that she interrupted her running to wipe her eyes with her fists so that she could verify that she was in fact seeing Father Raymond Curtis, dressed as a priest and in the belly of sobriety, walking from his presbytery in the direction of the house of Linus Gaynor. When she was satisfied that she was seeing the truth, she ran to the nearest house to report the event, bringing Dominic Bermingham, brother of Milo, out with her to the street, where they stood with bent necks and beating hearts at the sight which grew more distant by the second as Father Raymond Curtis's long legs took him quickly to his destination.

Outside Poule, he again found a small group of believers, just as many as had been there the last time he had passed that way, but on this occasion he looked upon them with pity as he felt sure that within minutes he would bring them the news that Linus Gaynor no longer wanted them to come and pray by his wall as the curing of Grainne Dearvla Feherty and the agoraphobic had been nothing more than the emergence of common sense. In contrast to his own garden, that of Gretchen Gaynor lay pristine despite the weather, and he promised himself that in addition to clearing away the rubbish in his presbytery he would also go and speak to Miss Aoife Quill bearing an irresistible apology and plead with her to come and again place her gifted hands on his deranged garden. But that was to be later. For now he pulled in air through his mouth until his chest sat up like a fat pigeon, and rapped on the wooden door of Poule.

When she opened it, Gretchen Gaynor stood with continued surprise at a day which had already brought her such unexpected pleasure. She was indeed pleased to see Father Raymond Curtis, as his absence had filled her with an uneasy feeling of unholiness, so she took him by the arm and led him to the kitchen, where she dispensed him some excellent chicken soup. 'I thought you had abandoned us forever,' she said to him.

'I only abandoned myself,' he answered, 'but I am back now.'

After he had devoured several cups of the brew, Father Raymond Curtis stood upright in the kitchen, so upright that his great head crashed against the lampshade, sending it whirling around and making every shadow in the room jump about the walls. Grabbing the swinging light, he apologised clumsily, almost falling backwards over his feet as he reversed to prevent his head taking a hammering. When order had been restored, he announced to Gretchen Gaynor that he would like to spend some moments alone with her husband. She quickly agreed to this, as it seemed to her that nothing could go wrong with the day, so she led him to the bottom of the stairs and left him on his own, watching him mount the steps lightly until he was standing outside Linus Gaynor's bedroom, his forefinger bent out in front of him ready to tap on the door. With that, Gretchen Gaynor returned to her kitchen where she started making some more chicken soup, intending to produce an exact replica of the potion which had brought her such good fortune that day.

Father Raymond Curtis did not remain for long in the bedroom of Linus Gaynor. Gretchen guessed that he could not have been there for more than ten minutes. When he returned to her he had a broad smile on his face and he moved as if to embrace her for an instant before pulling back at the last moment as he remembered who he was. 'I have very good news for you,' he said to her. 'You will no longer be troubled by crowds outside your door. Your husband has told me that they are to be sent away and ordered not to return. All of this business with Grainne Dearvla Feherty is just hocuspocus – nothing more than the illusions of a crazed woman. Your husband has no special healing powers. All he has is an ear willing to listen.' With that, and without even waiting to hear any response she might have, Father Raymond Curtis left the kitchen, where Gretchen Gaynor stood with a plucked chicken in her arms and a look of astonishment on her face.

When he reached the front garden, Father Raymond Curtis walked round to the concrete footpath where the group of lunatics stood, and announced to them they were to leave at once. This, he said, was a combined instruction from the Church and from Linus Gaynor himself, who had admitted that, though he had initially thought there might be something to it, he was now convinced that all of the rumours of his powers were false. The priest passed on Linus Gaynor's most sincere apologies but also his wish that he be left alone in peace to continue his life as best he could. With that he began to herd the crowd from off the concrete path and out on to the road, where they wandered like orphaned ducklings without knowing what was happening to them.

Father Raymond Curtis's dismissal of the believers had been seen by Meabh Slevin as she ran back to her house. The sight filled her with such uncontrollable rage that she ran to the priest shouting at him that he had gone too far this time and that he ought to be ashamed of his behaviour towards the bewildered. But he interrupted her in mid abuse, his enormous hands held out in front of him with the palms open, telling her that he was acting on the instructions of Linus Gaynor, and that from then on there were to be no more pilgrimages to his wall as there was nothing behind it which could offer the congregation anything in the way of a cure. 'This is a lie,' she yelled at him. But he assured her that he was telling the truth, a fact which could be verified by Gretchen Gaynor. When that had been done, Father Raymond Curtis found himself making a magnanimous apology. In the place of their faith in Linus Gaynor, he asked them to work with him again in the cause of poverty, which could be eradicated if they applied the same ardour which had seen their belief in Linus Gaynor burgeon into a sea of faith.

On his return to his presbytery Father Raymond Curtis set about cleaning the place. The disarray of the rooms angered him as if he had been burgled, even though he knew that he himself had been the villain. In all it took him two hours before the house was at all presentable, and he would later spend the occasional hour fixing smaller bits before the whole building was habitable again. He also went to the house of Miss Aoife Quill. She at first greeted him with a look of deathly indifference, but after he had spoken to her for several minutes he convinced her of the totality of his transformation. His accounts of the condition of his garden reduced her to near tears, and she accepted his offer of renewed employment.

That evening Father Raymond Curtis sat in the study of his presbytery, which had now been restored to the use for which it was originally intended, and wrote two letters. The first of them was to Darius Gaynor, informing him that the priest would be honoured to officiate at his wedding. The second letter was to his Bishop, who believed that the reports he had received of the condition of his wayward cleric had finally provided him with the reason he had looked for for so many years to throw him out of the priesthood entirely. But now Father Raymond Curtis wrote to him with the news that all was returning to normal, and that Linus Gaynor had not only disclaimed any ability to perform miracles but had done so partly because of the persistent opposition of Father Raymond Curtis. When he had finished the letter, he reread it several times, on each occasion increasing his admiration for himself and relishing the prospect that he could now begin again the work which he knew to be his real mission.

Chapter Ten

In the days before his marriage to Roberta Staunton, Darius Gaynor's stomach would not retain any of the food he put into it. He spent hours standing over the four-foot-deep hole he had dug in his temporary garden and into which they threw anything that would rot. There he would stand with his back to the house so no one could see the contents of his vomit or the upsetting sight of his face bent in anguish as he retched into the earth, trying as best he could to keep the noise to a minimum. On many occasions Roberta Staunton asked him if she should send for the doctor as she considered such a persistent illness to be more than just nerves, but he forbade her to do so, insisting that it was nothing more than a temporary virus which would pass. So they experimented with his food to see if there was anything which he could retain, and after some time they concluded that a combination of skipjacks and ugli fruit worked better than anything else.

When he was not bent over the hole in the ground, Darius Gaynor made several more trips to Poule. There he would engage only in flippant conversations with his mother before excusing himself and going to the room of Linus Gaynor to spend hours in long conversations which his mother could not make out, even with the ear she had trained over the years to snatch individual words from conversations in her husband's room. After these visits, her son would emerge in a state of quietness which she believed to be inappropriate for a man waiting to be married, so she asked him again if he was certain that he loved Roberta Staunton and he answered that he was.

On the morning of his wedding, Darius Gaynor dressed himself in the magnificent black trousers which had been lent to him for the day by his business friend Charles O'Morchu, who had added black satin stripes down the sides of the legs so that he would look like a film star when he promenaded along the streets of the capital. Charles O'Morchu had never needed a genuine excuse to dress like a gigolo for in his own mind he was the apple of many a woman's eye, but such was the deceitfulness of his imagination that it never occurred to him that he looked like an apprentice pimp. So he strode with his back straight and his head pinned back, the satin stripes of his trousers reflecting the light of the lamps along the dull streets which he liked to think of as boulevards, his pert waist enshrined in the azure cummerbund he had purchased by mail order from London. It had been a wrench for Charles O'Morchu to part with his beloved trousers so that Darius Gaynor could wear them on his wedding day, but he consented because of the depth of their friendship and the guarantee that he would receive an invitation to the occasion where he could remain close by his favourite garments to ensure their safety. 'I am very close to my trousers,' he said. 'Nothing would upset me more than to see harm come to them.'

Before they went to the church, everyone paid a visit of homage to Linus Gaynor, who lay as he had done for so many years, unable to move a muscle in congratulations or sorrow at the wedding of his eldest son. In a room full of people all talking among themselves, the father and son knew what was on each other's mind even though not a word could be spoken of the pact agreed between them on the day that Linus Gaynor consented to the marriage of his son to Roberta Staunton. They then went to the church, where Father Raymond Curtis recited the doxology of marriage and pronounced the couple man and wife to the tears of Gretchen Gaynor, who had spent much of the morning reminding Roberta Staunton to ignore the tragedy of Darius's destiny.

In the hours after the marriage, the Farmers' Hall rang to the sound of Milo Bermingham's violin and an accompanying ensemble of pipes and flautists. The music resounded across the streets and the fields, and crept into the room where Linus Gaynor lay in silence waiting for the return of his son the following day. After she had spent several hours with her guests, Gretchen Gaynor left the Farmers' Hall and went to sit with him. In her hand she carried a jug of Worcester Pearmain wine made especially by Loretta Mairead Siobhan Gaynor, who had foreseen that Linus Gaynor would not persist in his objections to the marriage of his son, and that when he relented and the wedding took place there would be need for plenty of wine.

That night when Darius Gaynor lay for the first time with his wife, she could tell by his abstracted air that something unknown to her was troubling him. In the previous weeks the eccentricity of his behaviour had worried her, for not only had he spent hours bent over the hole in the garden, but he had also shown scant regard for her presence – treating her sometimes as if she was nothing more than a temporary charwoman.

In all of that time, Roberta Staunton had played every card in her hand except one. She had tried to counteract his aloofness with a similar display of uninterest in his welfare, walking past him as he vomited into the abyss without a word of commiseration. When this failed to alert him to her discomfort, she tried flirtation, showing increasing interest in an older man who came to sell mussels and whelks and found himself the unwitting subject of her feigned attention. But still Darius Gaynor did not seem to notice her unease, so she tried anger as a weapon of despair, shouting at her fiancé as she had not done since the days when he failed to correctly complete his invoices for sultanas and ginger. But this had no effect on him either and merely served to make him more confusing in her eyes. She had begun to fear the very worst about his motives, namely that his love had died and the spirit which tortured him was its ghost, which was set to roam the halls of his mind in an interminable search for an exit and which might one day appear with the same violence as the demon which emerged from her father and poisoned every room of her childhood. The possibility that such a potential lay inside Darius Gaynor made her cry with ignorance.

But there was still one last thing which came to her salvation, one loyal ally which refused to desert her in the hours she lay awake beside her future husband, and that was her faith in him. From the chaos of her fears she summoned her conviction that Darius Gaynor was a good man, incapable of such chicanery, and this consoled her. But despite her reliance on this as her only reason to continue to love him, she never had the courage to ask him what troubled him, believing that to hope was better than to risk the bitter truth which might be revealed in the honesty of his reply. So she lay beside her husband on their wedding night, and the only actions which came from him were the accompaniments to whiskied snores which made her ears ache.

She turned her eyes away from his body so that they could peer out of the window of the hastily renamed Bridal Suite in the American Hotel. There was nothing to be heard in the night except the occasional bottle breaking as a reminder of the recent past. But hers was not the only pair of eyes which lay open that night. No more than a few hundred yards from where she lay as an untouched bride, Linus Gaynor looked up at the ceiling and noticed a new direction to the crack in the plaster which had taken five years to travel three feet above his head and whose course he had plotted like a diligent cartographer recording the source of the Nile. There he lay amid the overwhelming silence knowing that Darius would come to see him the following day as they had agreed, for he too had blinding faith in his son.

They say that the sky of the following morning brought with it the unmistakable omens of foreboding. It defied the signs given by the rosy dusk of the previous evening which had been interpreted by Felix McDaid, the gauger, as the precursor to a blue crisp morning, but it had not turned out that way. When she pulled back the curtains of her bedroom, Gretchen Gaynor could not help herself from shivering with an uncanny numbness in her bones that the day was an impostor placed over them by an evil hand which had snatched the rightful heir from the bosom of the night and put in its place a grey charlatan heavy with drizzle and arthritis which muted the cockerels and persuaded the hens that they should stay indoors lest their eggs be stolen from them. Although it was easy for him to say so in the certainty of hindsight, Father Raymond Curtis took one look at the sky on that morning and rushed straight to his diary. 'It is strangely dark this morning,' read the entry. 'I must remember to have my teeth seen to.'

When Darius Gaynor took his first look at the day, he was not surprised at what he saw, and as he ate the flummery specially made for him by Della Talbot he peered out the window of the breakfast room to see if there was anyone about. He ate alone, which came as a disappointment to Della Talbot. He explained his wife's absence as being caused by fatigue due to the rigours of the previous day, but the truth was that she had not fallen asleep until shortly before dawn, a sleep assisted by the absence of the cockerels, and so she lay unaware of the tragedy in the weather. Despite his compliments to Della Talbot on the quality of her oatmeal pudding, Darius Gaynor did not enjoy it in the slightest and forced himself to eat it only because there was nowhere near to dispose of it without being seen by the cook, who watched every move of his eating as if she were learning the craft herself. So he had no alternative but to summon a smile of satisfaction to his face and strain to keep it there until he could walk past Della Talbot and out on to the street.

He found the street even colder than it had looked from the window of the breakfast room in the American Hotel, and the clothes he had chosen were pitifully inadequate for the task of keeping him warm on such a morning. Chastened by the conditions, he walked quickly though in truth he was in no hurry to reach his destination, but he believed that to loiter in such weather would alert anyone who saw him to the fact that something was on his mind. At the pace he moved it took him only a few minutes to reach Poule, where the quietness of the building made him think that no one had risen yet. He knocked on the door with a gentleness made difficult because his arm shook with the cold, and in a few moments Gretchen Gaynor was standing in front of him, shocked by the sight of a new husband turning up at her door on the first morning of his marriage. They both walked to the kitchen, where she made him tea. 'I've come to say goodbye,' he said. 'I'm on my own because I couldn't wake Roberta.'

After he had spoken to his mother for some time, he left her in the kitchen and walked up the stairs to the bedroom of Linus Gaynor, who he found lying with his eyes open. Looking into them, Darius could see that his father had become an old man for the first time, his face bearing the exhaustion of his immobility and his heart tired of keeping him alive just so he could lie like a sarcophagus whose view of the world never changed. Darius turned the key in the door with the stealth of a burglar and returned to look again into his father's eyes. Between them there was once more the ease of friendship which had characterised Darius Gaynor's youth in the presence of his father. The friendship had returned when Darius had accepted the condition that, with all the intensity his eyelids could muster, his father had laid down for his consent to Darius and Roberta Staunton being married: that, in return for the attention that his father had lavished on him in his youth, Darius would end the dreadful torment of Linus Gaynor's life.

When he had finished, Darius Gaynor unlocked the door and returned to the kitchen. He told his mother that Linus Gaynor was sleeping and he did not wish to waken him, and with that he said goodbye and returned to the American Hotel. There he found his wife sitting in the breakfast room with Della Talbot, who had insisted on inflicting the remainder of her flummery on the bride, who looked equally unhappy with its taste. After she had finished, they drove back to the capital. They passed Poule on the way, and the house was as quiet as he had found it that morning.

Sometime between the moment they drove past Poule and the moment Darius Gaynor turned the key in their house in the capital, Linus Gaynor had been found in his bed and someone had run to the post office to dispatch a panicked telegram to Darius with the news that his father was dead. When he returned to Poule his mother took him in her arms and told him that Linus Gaynor must have died shortly after Darius had seen him that morning. By this time the house was full of wailing women, many of them his relatives, who confessed in rotation that they had always secretly known that the mystery of Linus Gaynor's survival was a fluke not a turning-point and they each in turn recited the incantations of lament which had become second nature to them all.

Darius Gaynor found his mother to be in a state of enormous calm. She told him of all the times she had spent alone with Linus Gaynor, their silence saturated with the spell of sorrow she felt for him, each of them knowing what the other was thinking, namely that Linus Gaynor just might have been a luckier man if he was dead rather than spending those incalculable days picking through the ash-heaps of other peoples' lives in search of justice. She told her son of the private happiness that Linus Gaynor had transmitted to her when he dreamt of the marriage of his eldest son, and despite her grief at having lost him she did not prevent herself from making the sign of the cross with earnest gesticulations at the grace of God for having let him live to see the wedding day. As he listened to his mother speak,

Darius Gaynor felt that he should have borne the terrible burden of the truth, but he did not have any feelings of guilt as he stood beside the body of his father, a white cloth wedged beneath its chin to stop it gaping, and from the peaceful corpse exuded the merciful vindication of what Linus Gaynor had asked his son to do.

Two days later the body of Linus Gaynor was taken from the house in a coffin made of specially darkened wood. On top of it lay a hastily made crucifix, its arms turned by Aloysius Bermingham on his untested lathe from the legs of his mother's precious Victorian whatnot as a token of his respect for Linus Gaynor, who had saved him from the pit of alcoholism with nothing more than the tenor of his silence. Lots had been drawn to select the pallbearers, but so many had been disappointed that Gretchen Gaynor agreed to the cortège circling the church three times in a clockwise direction so that more would be able to speak of the day they carried Linus Gaynor aloft, and also because of the pagan superstition, disguised in the clothes of Christianity, that such a motion round a sacred place soothed the path of the dead. From the church Linus Gaynor was taken to the graveyard, where it is said the larks fell silent as he passed, and where he was buried among the men whose early demise had been the ransom for his fame.

It was through the newspapers that Judge Olin Prescott learned of the death of Linus Gaynor. For eight years he had secretly locked himself into his office in the mornings to scan the obituaries for the names of accomplices and enemies, showing an equal lack of emotion whenever he came across a familiar name. It was only when he read of Linus Gaynor that he jumped from his chair

211

and roared at the top of his voice in anger, the noise cascading down through the building into every court-room and causing proceedings to be halted while bail-iffs went to check if another war had started. Judge Olin Prescott threw the newspaper on the floor and jumped on it for several moments before collapsing back into his chair in exhaustion and rage, mouthing filthy words of rancour at Linus Gaynor for having died before he was finished with him. 'You thieving dog,' he screamed, 'you selfish thieving dog. How dare you do this to me? How dare you insult me like this?'

When he emerged from his room, the Judge informed his petrified secretary that he was cancelling all his appointments for two days, and with that he pulled on his black cashmere coat. This was almost a foot too long for him, so that when he walked he looked as if he was rolling on wheels.

He drove from the capital but this time did not stop to look back at it. His speed on the awful roads was dangerous for anyone who came near him, and it was more by luck than by skill that he was not killed several times over on his journey. When he drove past Poule he refused to look at the building as a sign of the depth of the betrayal he felt at what had been done to him. He drove to the American Hotel and parked his car in the usual place, and within seconds word had reached Police Sergeant Donald Kilgallon that the Judge was back. The police officer immediately commenced another letter of resignation, but before he could word the address he saw the Judge march past his window having received directions to the cemetery, which was the only place he had any interest in seeing. When he saw him pass, Police Sergeant Donald Kilgallon slipped the piece of paper into the wastebasket without looking at it in case it brought him bad luck, and then he set out to stalk the Judge from a distance.

When Judge Olin Prescott found Linus Gaynor's grave, the frost still gripped the lumps of soil, for the sun could not shine past the church wall until late in the afternoon. Standing beside the mound of earth, the Judge felt himself become calm. The anger which had seized his heart that morning had fled, and in its place he could sense a peacefulness emerge as it occurred to him that no one had ever made him as angry as Linus Gaynor had done by the simple act of dying. No one had ever preoccupied him so much as this man, not even in the early days of his career when he considered righteousness a virtue and not a mask for deceit. Not even in those days of his outrageous disrespect when he had striven against the giants of a corrupt legal system and relished the task of unseating hypocrites had anyone held his attention hostage to the extent that Linus Gaynor had done. He did not know what he felt towards the dead man. It seemed that his head was a torrid pool of confusion. Inside it there was a mixture of respect and admiration, hate and jealousy, loneliness and despair. He could not pick out any one of them as being dominant, and slouching behind the leafless Russian vine, with his big arse sticking out as if attracted by the magnetic north, Police Sergeant Donald Kilgallon swore to himself that he saw Judge Olin Prescott crying by the grave of Linus Gaynor.

He was not incorrect in his observation, but he was in error in reporting that the Judge was crying because of the deep-seated love which he had for Linus Gaynor, a love which he could only reveal when the target of his authority was no longer touchable. This was not the case, for Judge Olin Prescott had long since practised the art of loving nothing but himself. What Police

213

Sergeant Donald Kilgallon saw was the evolution of the Judge into the phase of his life which he had always known would be the last, the period in which he would spend his days of retirement lying on the wicker divan with his pipe full of aromatic black German tobacco and his head sodden with the memories of a dissonant career – from the glory of its beginning to the bitter last day when he stood at the grave of Linus Gaynor as nothing more than a spent *apparatchik*. What the Police Sergeant saw from his makeshift hide were the final moments of the Judge's career, for when Judge Olin Prescott returned to the capital he went straight to his office, where it took him no more than five minutes to compose a letter of resignation to the Chancellor which formally ended twenty-eight years of persistent decline. When he had finished that he went out into the street to walk through the one thing that he loved.

The path to the cemetery was taken by many others in the weeks that followed. Douglas Bermingham, the brother of Milo, was best placed to see them from the tops of the sweet-chestnut trees he had been employed to cut back. He dangled from the limbs like a Balkan acrobat with nothing for safety but a length of electrical wire tied around his waist which would have sliced him in half if he had fallen. From there he observed the constant procession of mourners who came armed with coniferous bouquets until the grave of the deceased was no longer reachable. It was a procession which did not cease with time, and long after Douglas Bermingham had finished his surgery mourners still came in sizeable numbers and stood at the spot where Judge Olin Prescott had cried in betrayed isolation.

Father Raymond Curtis was among the most frequent visitors. He would come when it was dark or on market day, when his presence would not be so public. For despite the work which he was able to resume in the name of the poor, he never fully eradicated the feeling of inferiority he felt towards Linus Gaynor. Nor could he reject beyond argument that what Linus Gaynor had offered people was more nourishing than the hampers of vegetables and rabbit meat he was able to assemble with the charity of others.

Darius Gaynor came as well – on his own, always on his own, so he could speak with the honesty of the humanely guilty and derive sustenance from the spirit of the place.

But the most important of all the people who came were for the most part unknown to Linus Gaynor. They were the mothers of illegitimate children, the mortified bankrupts, the betrothed homosexuals, the unfaithful lovers, and the carriers of the tubercle bacillus. They came in such numbers that everyone knew it would only be a matter of time before one of them swore on the New Testament that Linus Gaynor had the gift of intercession. But for the moment it was enough for them to stand by his grave for some moments and then walk away in the faith that time would fulfil their prayers.